"River Raisin Richie" is library approved for elementary and middle school readers. Author Tom Bajkiewicz, a charter member of the Monroe Area Story Tellers of S. E. Michigan, is available for book presentations or story telling engagements. Contact Tom at riverraisinrich@provide.net

RIVER RAISIN RICHIE

by

Thomas A. Bajkiewicz

Copyright © 2003 by Thomas A. Bajkiewicz

ISBN 0-7414-1730-8

The locations and places in Monroe are real and historically correct.

Published by:

519 West Lancaster Avenue
Haverford, PA 19041-1413
Info@buybooksontheweb.com
www.buybooksontheweb.com
Toll-free (877) BUY BOOK
Local Phone (610) 520-2500
Fax (610) 519-0261

Printed in the United States of America

Printed on Recycled Paper

Published September 2003

Acknowledgments

Dedicated to our grandchildren, Ruth, Hannah, Joshua and Maxwell.

My most Heartfelt THANKS to:

My wife, Kay, partner in all my wild schemes.

Our children, Christopher, Pamela, David, Catherine and Dr. Timothy, who were a joy to watch grow up and become leaders because they were readers.

All the manuscript readers; Margo, Ruth, Cindy and Stella, who offered suggestions and encouragement.

A special thanks to Nikki for her creative Writing Class, punctuations and paragraphing.

A very special thanks to Dr. Bob for smoothing out many of the rough spots and helping it flow.

And to all who still have the wonder of a 'Richie.'

LIST OF ADVENTURES

1

THE TRAIL

Richie sat on the curb, his scuffed high top boots in the roadway. His face was cupped in both hands, elbows rested on his knees. The adventure had started out so exciting, but now the six year old was fighting back tears, though a few had escaped and were slowly streaming down his cheeks. "Big boys don't cry," he thought to himself. "Big boys don't get lost either," he added to his thought.

The mission, the great adventure, had begun that morning when he found the quarter in the grass by the curb in front of his house, actually gramma's house.

They now lived in the Spencer family home in an old Monroe neighborhood of stately two storied clapboard houses, built just a few paces apart, most with wide, covered porches that spanned the whole front.

Richie remembered that he and his mom had lived in Ann Arbor, the home of the University of Michigan, thirty-five miles northwest of Monroe. He had spent his days playing in the tiny two-room apartment in the back of mom and dad's Art and Rare Books shop in the town's business district, which seemed to weave in and out of the sprawling University campus.

Richie clearly recalled overhearing mom and gramma talking, during one Sunday visit, while sitting at the table in gramma's kitchen. Mom had expressed concern about how expensive it was to live in Ann Arbor. The bookshop wasn't profitable enough to maintain itself and pay the mortgage on the suburban house purchased before Richie's birth.

Richie was barely old enough to understand that his father, a news photographer for one of the local papers, had gone to cover the war in Korea. The war had been over for several years, but he was still missing.

Gramma had suggested they move to Monroe to live with her and grampa. She and grampa would be glad to have their company. Richie could attend the new Riverside Elementary School, a short walk across the Roessler Street Bridge to the corner of Elm Street. Mom could commute to her bookshop in Ann Arbor on the new I-75 and I-94 Expressways, staying over in the shop during bad weather or a long, tiring, workday.

Now here he was, he thought, sitting on the curb, unsure of the way home, but not exactly lost.

Earlier that morning, Richie knew, from trips with gramma, the neighborhood store was three blocks down and two over. He just knew he was plenty old enough to go there by himself. Just to be sure he could find his way back, he had the piece of chalk he found on grampa's old workbench in the garage where he played. He remembered reading how Daniel Boone had blazed a trail; nicked trees with his axe, so others could follow him to new lands in Kentucky. Gramma probably would not allow him to take the axe. The last time he used it, it felt a lot better to stand than sit for a few days. The stump of the plum tree near the back fence would always be a painful reminder. Marking the trees with grampa's chalk would blaze a nice trail. He put the quarter in his pocket, the chalk in one hand and his stick, which served as his Daniel Boone model long rifle, in his other for protection.

He set out for the store with thoughts of chocolate deliciously melting in his mouth. He found the store right where he knew it would be, and to make sure of the trail, he marked almost all the trees along the way. He was so excited during the journey; his usual limp could hardly be noticed.

Unfortunately when he turned the corner and saw the store, he forgot about marking any more trees and ran the rest of the way.

On the way home he ate the chocolate. He had not gone too far before beginning to wonder if he had started out in the right direction. He stood on the corner, looked up and down the street, but saw no chalk marked trees. He began to panic and wanted to run. Instead, he decided to sit down and think it over, like he remembered grampa would do.

He looked at the chalk in his hand. It reminded him of grampa. He liked helping grampa. When grampa fixed things, he always took the time to show Richie how to use the proper tools. They built different kinds of kites, and toys. Richie liked building model airplanes, helping glue in the tiny pieces that grampa complained were so small his new glasses didn't help at all. The best times, he remembered were when grampa took Richie out to the airport where everyone knew grampa and they would go flying in a small airplane. Richie always sat on a pile of cushions in the back seat strained against the seat belt with his nose stuck against the window for the whole flight. He sure did miss grampa.

He was sitting on the curb, deep in thought until he heard heavy footsteps. He turned his head as Percy, the mailman, dropped his bag, ruffled Richie's curly hair and sat down on the curb next to him. "Hey Richie" Percy said as he took a long swig from a bottle of Nehi Orange, "What are you doing here?" Richie was fighting back the tears valiantly as he explained his planned mission and, though he felt he was not lost, he could not seem to find his chalk blazed trail. Percy took a few small sips of orange, capped the bottle and stuck it in his mailbag. "Well," Percy said, as he pointed up the street, "Now I know what those white X's are on the other side of those trees. Percy stood, picked up his bag and said, "C'mon Richie, I'll walk you to the corner where you can see your house."

A few minutes later, a very somber boy slipped in the back door that opened into the kitchen. The smell of baking bread filled the room. Gramma, scrubbing vegetables at the sinkboard, glanced at Richie as she worked. "Where have you been, Richie?" gramma asked casually.

"Oh, just out front and down the street a little ways," Richie answered. Gramma raised an eyebrow as she turned toward him.

"Go wash your hands and face for lunch," she said.

Richie went into the bathroom and pulled the cord to switch on the bare bulb overhead.

Before he turned on the water, he glanced in the mirror of the medicine cabinet over the sink. The corners of his mouth were smudged with chocolate. When he finished washing, he went into the kitchen, sat down, picked up his sandwich and took a big bite.

"Did we have any mail, Richie?" Gramma asked coolly. Richie smiled as he chewed. She knew.

2

GOING HOME

Richie limped across the street with the other kids, shielded from the traffic by the considerable size of the crossing guard. He frequently glanced at the stick laying in the parking lot of Danny's Market across the street from Riverside School. He hoped none of the other kids would beat him to it. It was a beauty. Slightly longer than he was tall, round and smooth, yellow with one end showing the ragged bits of a break. "Looks like a broomstick," he decided, but now it was his, a magic staff. Before he left the parking lot, three assassins, all in black, faces hooded except for their eyes, barred his way. He, the wise old karate master, fought them, twirling the staff, turning and jumping. Their swords, knives and staffs littered the parking lot before they fled.

He retrieved his book bag and went back to the corner. The traffic moved like a surging sea. He was Moses, robed, his curly dark hair shining white, and his long beard rustling in the wind. He watched for the green light, thrust out his arms, staff held high. The rushing waters parted as he led his people across.

He carefully followed the native guide along the jungle path. Ahead, the Roessler Street Bridge, named after the early explorer Street, he guessed, spanned the rushing

River Raisin coursing through the gorge thousands of feet below. Using his trusted staff, he carefully tested the aged ropes and rotted planks of the teetering, swaying bridge. The piece of chalk, from grampa's workbench, saved the day. He carefully marked each step so none of the bearers carrying the supplies would break through and fall to their deaths far below. After again becoming Moses, parting the waves at the Front Street Sea, and crossing over, he almost passed the huge rock that stood near the walk. Still holding his chalk, he began to write, slowly, carefully. It would have to last forever. In history class today, they had studied the Rosetta Stone. Someone having lunch in the desert among the rocks discovered it in Egypt a long time ago. It had a story carved in several languages that helped translators read the script on the Pyramid tombstones. The chalk inscribed the complete alphabet, capital and small letters, and numbers from one to ten. Now, if the aliens came and destroyed everything, there would be the Richie Rock so books could be read and people could count.

Further down the street, he came upon an archeological treasure trove by the curb. A huge pile of good stuff, most broken beyond use, but the big TV box made a great lifeboat. He sat in the box, his staff now a mast. A piece of newspaper wasn't much of a sail, but it was better than nothing. He spent the next few minutes reading last weeks comics, turning the sail around and reading the page on the other side. On the inside flap of the box, he chalked the many days he had drifted across the barren sea. He was thirsty and starving, all the rations gone except the chocolate kiss Sarah had given him at lunch. Some of the girls, and especially Sarah, had this funny look in their eyes when he was around. They liked to touch his curly hair, tan cheeks and give him part of their lunch and candy. He looked up the street, looked down at the piece of chocolate, tore off the wrapper and popped it into his mouth.

"Rescue Ship, Ahoy!" bellowed the forward watch in the bow. "Uh-oh…" Richie thought, gramma was walking briskly toward him with fire in her eyes.

"Let's see," he thought, "would she believe why I'm late if I told her everything that happened?" He shook his head. "I wonder if I'm going to miss supper tonight?" He looked up and smiled, "Hi gramma, nice day for a walk, isn't it?"

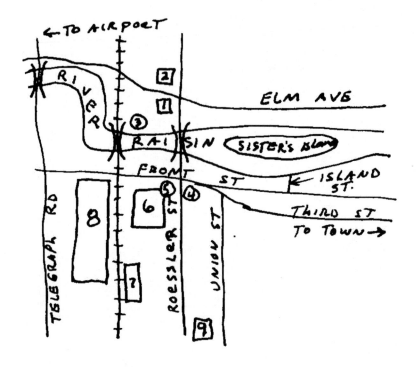

-Richie's MAP NOT To Scale-
1. Riverside School
2. Danny's MARKET
3. WATER TANK
4. Richie's Rock
5. REX, The dog
6. MONROE CASTINGS
7. R.R. STATION
8. MONROE LUMBER
9. CAIRNS Field.

3

THE RIVER

Richie carefully put one foot in front of the other. He held the metal detector, which others mistook for a worn out mop, close to the ground, slowly sweeping it back and forth. He had to clear the Roessler Street Bridge of land mines before Sarah, her brother Syl and the other kids crossed. It was a dangerous job. He hoped Sarah would know the risks he had to take. The safety of the civilians was his mission. Richie was so engrossed in his work, he didn't know anyone else was around until his book bag was snatched from his free hand and went sailing over the bridge railing. He turned to find Leroy Marlow chuckling and pointing to the river. His mine detector went over the rail next. Richie ran to the rail as it splashed into the water and began to drift with the fast current, the water level having been raised by heavy spring rains. Leaning against the bridge rail, Richie could see his book bag on the riverbank, not more than a yard from the edge of the water. It had not gone into the river. He raced around the end of the rail and carefully picked his way down the incline to retrieve the bag. He heard an ominous chuckle, turned to see Leroy racing down the bank, arms out stretched. "Get ready to take a swim, Richie," Leroy exclaimed. Richie stood frozen, but only for a moment. Leroy rushed toward him. In his mind, Richie clearly saw an illustration in the judo book he had found in grampa's old

Navy footlocker. He waited until the very last instant, until Leroy was one step away, and then Richie made his move. He swung his left foot well past his firmly planted right. It worked. Leroy missed with his intended rush and tripped over Richie's extended right leg. There was a big splash. Leroy was in the water and the current was sweeping him downstream. He was thrashing and struggling; then, Richie knew- Leroy couldn't swim.

Richie reacted by running along the bank and under the bridge toward a huge tree on the other side he had noticed just yesterday. Beside the tree lay the branch Richie needed. He scooped it up, ran to the river's edge and thrust it out toward Leroy's outstretched hands. Leroy grasped the branch. Richie dug in his heels and the force of the current did the rest, swinging Leroy into the shallows beside the bank. Leroy clambered up, puffing and spitting, and then rested his hands on his knees. After he caught his breath, Leroy looked up, gave Richie a menacing look and growled "I'm going to rip you apart for this, Richie!" He started to move toward Richie when his eyebrows raised and his mouth fell open. He had looked past Richie, suddenly turned, scrambled up the slope and ran away as fast as he could. Richie looked back to see what had scared Leroy off. Lining the bridge rail were more than a half dozen people including Sarah, her brother Syl and other classmates. There was also a man with a camera.

Richie ran back under the bridge, snatched up his book bag, climbed up the slope and headed for home. All he could think about was what gramma would say, or worse, would do; when she found out he was down by the river. He imagined her now, wagging her finger and shaking her head.

Richie stood quietly by the back door waiting for his racing heart and rapid breath to slow. He opened the door and walked past gramma setting the dinner table. He tried to act calm as he headed for the stairs and the safety of his room. Gramma had stopped what she was doing, staring at him. He could feel her eyes on the back of his head; the tall mirror alongside the front door ahead confirmed it. "Richie, come back here," Gramma said.

Richie turned, put on his innocent face and took a deep calming breath. "What's wrong Gramma?" Richie asked.

"That's what I would like to know, young man," Gramma said, as she crossed her arms, definitely a bad sign.

"Everything is fine; I just wanted to change clothes and get my homework done before dinner," he said. Then he asked, "How was your day?" His innocence filled eyes focused on a point just above her forehead. He did not want to look her in the eye. Gramma raised one eyebrow, slowly shook her head and went back to her work. Richie plodded up the stairs wondering if she already knew something. "How did she do that?" he muttered to himself.

He rushed through his homework, which was easy. All the schoolwork was easy. Reading wasn't work. He smiled as his eyes slowly swept over the bookcases filling his room. His dad had stocked these shelves when his dad was a kid. He liked to think he did it just for him. His favorite books were the Hardy Boy's mysteries and books about flying airplanes. He loved to sprawl on his bed, next to the window, and be swept away by words.

Since Richie's earliest years, there was always someone; mom, dad, a friend or one of the college students that continually hung around the bookstore, who was willing to read to him. He spurned the usual toys that toddlers played with in favor of books. Books were much more interesting, even the ones with few pictures. The customers always had to be careful to avoid tripping over Richie as he lay on the carpeting in one of the aisles, carefully turning pages in a book whose cover had aroused his curiosity. He learned to read before he was five and could not read enough. He read everything that passed before him: cereal boxes, soup cans, recipes, how-to-directions and the comics in the Monroe Evening News, his favorites being Red Ryder, Captain Easy and Donald Duck.

His play was drawn from the books mom was always bringing home from her shop plus others he found at the Dorsch Library with gramma every Thursday. Reading with mom or gramma, he rescued fair damsels with Lancelot as a Knight of the Round Table in the service of King Arthur; stood on the sea washed decks of the Pequod, hunting the great white whale, Moby Dick; stepped off the Mayflower at Plymouth Rock with the pilgrims; celebrated the signing of the Declaration of Independence in Philadelphia by ringing the Liberty Bell; rode with Paul Revere to warn that the British were coming; fought the redcoats at Lexington; carved out homesteads with the pioneers; plodded along wagons heading west to California; shivered in the frigid Alaskan wilderness prospecting for gold; soared over the wind swept sands of Kitty Hawk in the first powered flight of the Wright Brother's Flyer; battled the Red Baron with a bi-plane fighter in the skies of France during the First World War and flew the Atlantic Ocean from New York to Paris, France with Charles Lindberg in a tiny single engine plane called the "Spirit of St. Louis."

He was reading about the mysterious disappearance of Amelia Earhart flying across the pacific in 1937 when he heard the front doorbell. He went to the door of his room and tried to hear what gramma was saying to a man whose voice Richie couldn't recognize. "Richie, would you come down please?" Gramma called out. "Please," she had said. Gramma had said "Please," in her singsong voice. "Oh, Oh!" he thought. Fear gripped Richie like a chokehold. He crept down the stairs on tiptoes reluctantly.

A man, dressed nice with a shirt and tie was sitting on the couch. Richie thought he looked familiar. "Of course," Richie thought, "it was the man on the bridge with the camera!" Gramma was standing near the living room window reading the front page of the Monroe Evening News. Her face was serious. Something bad must have happened. He was afraid to ask.

"Richie, were you by the river today?" Gramma leveled her eyes on him.

"Well, yes, sort of, Gramma. I had to get my book bag that fell over the rail."

Gramma motioned Richie over, turning the paper toward him. The headlines read 'BOY SAVES FRIEND FROM RIVER'. There were pictures of Leroy in the water, Richie extending the branch to pull him out and Leroy saying something to Richie, probably thanks for saving him. Gramma knelt down and smothered Richie in a big hug. "I'm so proud of you, Richie," Gramma beamed, small tears forming in the corner of her eyes. All Richie could think of was what Leroy would do to him the next time they met. Worse yet, that everyone would think he and Leroy were friends. "Yuck!"

4

THE DIG

Dr. Richie, famous archeologist and explorer threw open the side door of the garage and stepped out into the back yard. Dressed in safari shorts, shirt and Sears and Roebuck bog stomping boots, he carried grampa's old pith helmet under his left arm and a long handled shovel in the opposite hand. In his imagination the backyard became the shimmering sands of the desert, which beckoned him with the promise of discovery. He had standing orders from the authorities (gramma) that all digs would be conducted along the great wall otherwise known as the back fence. He fell to his work like the professional he was, carefully placing the dirt on the old shower curtain as strongly suggested by the authorities (gramma). It did make for a neat pile, especially when it was to be put back in the hole, that is, the dig. Richie briefly recalled the gas meter reader falling in one of his early digs near the back of the house. It took three pieces of gramma's hot apple pie and a pot of coffee to cool an angry gas man and compensate for the dirty smudges on his uniform. Richie rested in the hole, already over three feet deep according to his yardstick. He took several sips of water from his army canteen, and then continued digging. A few pieces of broken pottery and old bottles with flared mouths turned up. One corked bottle, sadly without a genie, had a scrawled note inside made unreadable by moisture that had leaked in.

The dig was well over four feet deep when he found the first bone. He pulled the old paintbrush from his back pocket to carefully dust it. The Richie museum had its first artifact. A quick glance to check the back window confirmed that gramma had not been watching. There was still too little evidence of the find of the century to get her excited prematurely. Back in the garage, he put on Gramma's gardening gloves and grabbed his little sand shovel and a burlap potato sack. He checked the back window before stepping out into the yard. Gramma was probably watching her soaps, like she did most afternoons. Dr. Richie carefully excavated the bones, dusted them, half filling the sack. He checked the back window to see if he was observed before shouldering the artifacts.

The back door was opened slowly, a wide eye peering around the edge, checking to see if the kitchen was empty. Quietly, one step at a time, he carried the sack down into the basement and gently placed it on his worktable, an old door supported by stacked cement blocks. He filled a pail with water in the washtubs; then, using a sponge, carefully cleaned the bones, arranging them in order on his table. Stepping back, he smiled in deep satisfaction.

The smile faded at the sound of footsteps and the back door being opened. "Richie, lunch!" Gramma called out the open back door. He stood motionless and listened as gramma's steps moved overhead back into the kitchen. More time was needed to confirm the find before it could be announced to the world. The best thing would be for gramma to think he was still out in the yard. He then snuck up the stairs, opened and slammed the back door, noisily tramping into the kitchen. He slid onto a chair and started to reach for his sandwich.

"Richie, go wash. Your hands should be filthy after playing in the dirt," gramma said.

Richie looked down; his hands were clean. If he said they were, gramma might want to know why; so he went into the bathroom, ran the water, and rattled the towel holder.

He was munching his sandwich when Gramma asked how the dig was going. He could hardly hold back from announcing his find. He did mention the old bottles and broken pottery, but nothing about the bones. "If only she knew," he thought, as he tried to appear calm. After they had finished lunch, Richie excused himself and went up to his room. He filled a small box with a bottle of Elmer's glue, a roll of wire, black electrical tape, pliers and a knife. He made it down the stairs and almost past the living room when gramma turned from the TV, saw the box, and asked, "What are you up to, young man?"

"Just going down to the basement to put together . . . some models," Richie answered.

"Models? What models?" gramma asked.

"That was the wrong answer," thought Richie, his mind racing. "Just some stuff I'm making up," He said while smiling and, thinking "The truth will set you free."

"Alright Richie, just remember, no sawing. You need all your fingers," Gramma said as she turned back to the TV.

Using the glue, tape and wire, he connected bones until a figure had emerged. The black electrical tape contrasted very nicely with the white bones. He was putting an extra wind of wire on one large joint when his hair stood straight up and his eyebrows arched all the way to his hairline. Gramma had slipped quietly down the stairs and had given an earth-shattering scream loud enough to rattle the bones. "It's Freddie! It's Freddie! Richie, what have you done?' Gramma screamed.

Richie stood wide-eyed, unable to move as Gramma covered her face, sobbing softly. She sat down heavily on the stairs, drying her eyes with the corners of her apron. "Oh Richie, what have you done?"

Gramma held out her arms. Richie went into them hesitantly. She pointed to the skeleton, wired and taped, standing proudly on the table. "Richie, that was the best, and only dog we ever had. He was your father's best friend, went everywhere with him, even played football with him. Someone, one of the neighbors we think, poisoned poor old Freddie. We gave him a fitting burial in the back yard. I forgot all about him, until now." Gramma gave Richie a big hug. "Now, go put him back."

Richie removed all the tape and wire, put the bones in a plastic bag and sealed it. He carried it out to the yard and laid it reverently to rest in the hole. The bottle with the note, surely from his dad to Freddie, was placed at the head. He dumped the dirt back in the hole, tamped it down, stepped back and thought of a proper service to dignify Freddie. A bouquet of dandelions was collected and laid on the grave. He snapped to attention, saluted, holding the salute until he had finished humming taps. He collected all his equipment, put everything away, and headed toward the back door. The smell of macaroni and cheese, with tomatoes, filled the air. "My favorite," thought Richie, "especially since me and gramma invented it."

5

THE DETECTIVE

The children had all filed out of Riverside School with the closing bell. The parking lot was full of cars, more so than usual. Small groups of parents stood around; no one spoke. Gramma was there, her old coat on, apron hanging out, as if she had been in a hurry to get to the school. She ignored Richie when he asked her what was wrong, took him by the hand and dragged him over the Roessler Street Bridge and headed for home. The river was high and the water rushed by just below the walkway. Richie remembered the news programs last night talking about the river reaching flood stage today. When they got in the house, gramma went down on one knee and hugged Richie so hard he thought she was going to break his ribs. She was softly sobbing. She dabbed at her eyes with the hankie she carried in her apron. She pushed him out to arms length and shook him, then said in a frightening tone like distant thunder, "Richie, if I ever hear of you playing down by the river you won't be able to sit down for a week! Do you hear me?" Richie was terrified, his eyes wide and unblinking. "Yes, gramma," he answered, then softly asked, "But why?" Gramma stood, turned away, remembering similar tragedies through the years. She continued to dab the hankie at her eyes. "You know Sylvester, Sarah's little brother. He was last seen on Island Street and his coat was found by the river's edge. Everyone, including the police, have been looking for him or for... for... any sign of him," she sniffled. Richie started to walk away in deep thought. He knew Syl. Sarah usually brought him along when they played. He was afraid of the water and would never go near the river. Richie furrowed his brow. This will be a chance to practice detecting, like Sherlock Holmes. He believed he could find Syl. He turned and smiled. "Gramma, can I go over to the Sanders? Sarah could probably use some company. She must be worried and upset." Gramma came over and hugged him. "That is so nice Richie. You can go, but straight there and the long way, away from the river." Richie ran up the stairs to his room. He dumped everything out of his army knapsack and began to collect his equipment. He had a flashlight, magnifying glass, fingerprint powder and brush, notebook and pencils and his canvas rain hat. He could fashion the hat with safety pins into one like Sherlock Holmes wore, which was called a deer slayer. He put on his old jeans, bog stomping boots and windbreaker, and shrugged his arms through the straps of his pack on the way down the stairs. He came up on gramma, busying herself at the sink, looking out the back window, deep in thought. He hugged her from behind and turned toward the door. "I'll be home for supper, Gramma," Richie said over his shoulder. He went out the front door and turned right toward the corner, the long way to Sarah's house. Stopping at the alley in the next block, he put on his Sherlock hat, and then ran, crouching behind the alley fences and cutting through yards, until he came out on Front Street. Richie walked fast, but not fast enough to attract attention, especially at Island Street where it led to the river at the point Syl had last been seen.

A great number of footprints by the river's edge led in all directions. Richie ignored these and went to a trimmed bush a few yards from the sidewalk. Whenever the kids played here, they always hung their coats, jackets or sweaters on this bush. He found a broken branch about three feet above the ground. It was the right height and the break was fresh. Clumps of tall weeds bending and swaying on the riverbank confirmed the wind to be strong and steady toward the river. Syl shed his coat on this warm spring day, hung it on the bush, the branch broke, the coat fell on the ground and the wind rolled it to the waters edge. Syl would not have gone down to retrieve it because the rushing water frightened him. Then again, he may have forgotten about the coat, and just went on his way. On the sidewalk just ahead of the coat bush were the chalked squares of a hopscotch pattern. Richie looked under the bush for the coffee can in which their marker stones were kept. Every player had a special stone. Syl's was missing. Richie moved to the end of the squares. The last, or home square, was empty. He carefully looked in the grass, on one side, then the other. He found Syl's stone in the little furrow trimmed back along the edge of the sidewalk. Syl would have left his stone in the home square to show he had finished the hop. Someone walking by may have kicked it off the walk. Richie smiled. He thought, "Syl had gone this way and was not lost in the river. Where could he be?" He moved off slowly down the street, looking for new signs

      Richie spotted the swings in the Gardner's yard where all the kids were welcome to play, Syl loved to swing. Richie approached the swings from the side, careful not to disturb any evidence. He closely examined the point where the swing chains were hung on the eyebolts of the frame. A lot of rain had fallen over the past few days and everyone he knew hadn't been allowed out to play. The eyebolts and chains all had a thin crust of rust except the end swing; the one Syl always used. The eyebolts were shiny where the chain rubbed. Richie walked past the swings on the grass and avoided the bare ground under the seats. Syl usually dismounted from the swing with a jump on a slow upswing. The wet sand had two small shoe imprints. Using his magnifying glass, notebook and pencil, Richie studied the shoeprints and made a sketch. The right sole print showed a cut diagonally across the toe. Richie snapped his fingers as he remembered. Last week Syl had stepped on a broken bottle bottom and fell, twisting his ankle. 'Doctor Richie' had examined Syl's foot to be sure it had not been cut. It had been his right foot.

Richie went west on Front Street toward the corner where the Monroe Castings Plant stood. He crossed the street and started to pat Rex, the bronze dog statue. Every kid in town hugged or patted Rex every time they passed by. Richie pulled his hand back before he touched Rex's head. Rex, a bigger than life Labrador, as the story is told, was the foundry owner's beloved companion, sealed in bronze at his passing and forever immortalized. Rex was polished every morning by one of the foundry janitors. Any fingerprints on Rex would be fresh. All the while Richie studied Rex, he could have sworn Rex cocked his head and wagged his tail. Richie dusted Rex's head with the fingerprint powder. A single small handprint appeared. At the request of the police, all the children were being kept in their homes while the search was being made for Syl. The handprint was the right size. It could be Syl's. Richie had not seen any kids out on the streets. He looked toward the west. Now he had a good idea where Syl might be. Richie patted Rex and hurried toward the railroad tracks. Was the foundry owner's dog really inside, like all the kids said? Someday, he thought, he would invent a portable X-ray machine and find out. Behind the foundry was a lot where they dumped casting sand that was used for making molds. Adjoining that were some trees that had grown into a small dense grove. He reached the railroad tracks, turned south, walked past the railroad station, circled the grove and looked around casually to make certain no one saw him enter the trees. He walked to one of the larger trees, reached up and pulled a piece of broomstick nailed to the tree with a wire attached. A rope ladder fell from above. He climbed the ladder through a trapdoor and pulled the ladder up after him. He stood on a small deck nestled in the large branches. Above, a rough wooden ladder reached a small hut. Climbing slowly and quietly, he reached the door of the hut and cautiously peered in. There, peacefully sleeping, lay Sylvester.

Richie sat leaning against the doorframe watching the steady rise and fall of Syl's chest in the smooth rhythm of sound sleep. Looking west across the railroad tracks was the Monroe Lumber Company. Workers were busily unloading rail flat cars of fresh new lumber, the woodsy smell carried to the tree house on the wind. His eyes followed the tracks north past the Penn Railroad Station, across Front Street, over the Railroad Bridge spanning the rushing brown torrent of the rain-swollen river. Directly across on the opposite bank stood the water tower and his Riverside School. He had found Syl and felt on top of the world in his tree house, while he scanned his neighborhood, the kingdom of Roessler on the Raisin. He smiled. It felt so good to be up here, but it was time to go.

After they had climbed down and drawn the ladder up out of sight in the tree, they circled the grove, emerged near the railroad tracks, and went home.

"Syl, people have been worried about you; they think you fell in the river." "Richie, I didn't go by the river. When I couldn't find my coat anywhere, I thought I left it in the tree house. When I got there and couldn't find it, I got worried, because mom just bought me that coat. I didn't want to have to tell her I lost it. I laid down and must have fallen asleep," Syl replied.

"I don't think you should worry about your coat, someone found it by the river. I think when they see you, they'll forget all about your coat," Richie said as they turned up Syl's street. Richie added, "Syl, remember, the tree house is secret. The truth is I ran into you in the neighborhood. That is the truth, isn't it?"

"Yes, Richie. Do you think I'll get a spanking?" Syl asked.

Richie smiled, "No, not today anyway. You might get grounded, but I think everyone will be really glad to see you."

When they got close to Syl's house, a trio of policemen stood on the front walk talking and gesturing.

They all suddenly stopped and turned as Richie and Syl approached. Sarah, sitting on the porch steps, stood as she cried out her brother's name and rushed down the porch stairs. The nearest policeman looked up at Syl, back at the photo in his hand, and asked, "Sylvester, is that you?" Syl nodded. The policeman scooped him up and ran up the stairs into the house. Inside, shouting and cheering erupted.

Sarah was still standing out front with Richie. She slowly moved closer and her face softened. Her eyes glazed over with the same look she had last week when she picked up a newborn puppy and kissed it on the nose. Richie wrinkled his nose, not knowing what she was going to do. She took his hand and they swung hands, back and forth, at least a half dozen times. She then gave his hand a good squeeze, let go, and ran into the house. Richie headed for home. He had chill bumps running up and down his spine, small beads of sweat on his brow and a queasy stomach. "Why," he asked himself, "does Sarah do that to me?"

Richie came in the back door as gramma was cooking something that smelled heavenly. He felt famished. Detecting, he decided, was hard work. Gramma glanced at him as she took the roaster out of the oven. "Any news about Sylvester?" She asked.

"Yes gramma, he showed up at home. He's okay."

"Thank God" she said with a sigh of relief. "Go wash up, Richie, mashed potato and hamburger hash for supper," gramma said as she filled three plates, for gramma, mom and Sherlock Richie.

Richie smiled as he imagined Holmes puffing on his pipe and nodding agreement at Watson's closing remark, "I say, Master Richie, well done!"

Rex, The Monroe Castings Mascot, standing guard.

.

6

THE 4TH OF JULY

Richie put the flag in the holder on the post and hung the red, white and blue bunting across the front of the porch. The fourth of July was finally here. Everyone was preparing for the parades, picnics and especially the evening fireworks display out at the Monroe County fairgrounds tomorrow. A ride out to the fairgrounds had been arranged with Mr. and Mrs. Mackay so Gramma and Richie could enjoy the aerial display. Mom was at an art fair in Ann Arbor selling books.

Richie was always up at the crack of dawn. In the spirit of the early patriots, he marched around the yard with his homemade flintlock rifle, ever ready to fight off any stray British soldiers who might threaten the signing of the Declaration of Independence inside the hall he guarded in Philadelphia. He had safety pinned three corners into his floppy rain hat, wore a faded denim shirt, an old pair of pants cut off below the knee, and long socks that were a little short and exposed the upper part of his shins.

He was patrolling the north fence when something trailing a thin string of smoke flew by and just missed his head. The explosion in the grass a few feet away made him jump back in terror. An ominous laugh came from the large tree just beyond the fence. Another object sailed toward him; causing him to drop his rifle, cover his ears and flatten himself, face first, against the fence. After the bang, as the smoke puff of the firecracker drifted across the yard, Richie ran for the side door of the garage. Once inside, Richie peaked back around the doorframe. He could see Leroy and two of his bully friends in the tree next door. A cigarette hung in Leroy's mouth with which he was lighting firecrackers, throwing them into the alley and Richie's yard. They taunted Richie, calling him "chicken little" and they ridiculed his patriot's uniform. "Look," Leroy said, "He thinks he's a soldier." He threw another firecracker and laughed as Richie ducked back into the garage. Richie knew that fireworks were illegal in Michigan. He also knew that some of the older boys, with cars, would collect money from kids like Leroy, drive the twenty miles or so to the Ohio state line and bring back a load of fireworks, if the State Police didn't catch them. Leroy and his buddies had climbed down from the tree and went into the alley. They were putting lit firecrackers under cans and the explosion tossed them high in the air.

Richie put on his foil-covered knight's armor. He also had, for added safety, put on his flying helmet and goggles. He had read how dangerous fireworks could be and he was taking no chances. Every year in July since he could remember, gramma reminded him not to touch anything that looked like a firecracker should he find one. She mentioned that when she was younger and worked as a nurse, she could never forget the youngsters she treated, victims of illegal fireworks. Crouching, he sneaked along the fence to the back gate. The crack where the gate hung slightly open against the hook allowed him, unseen, to watch Leroy and his friends. Leroy was scrounging in the trash for more missiles to launch, found a mustard jar, lit a firecracker thicker than his thumb and placed the jar over it. All the boys scattered for cover. Many seconds passed, quietly. The awaited explosion never happened. Leroy crept from behind a trashcan and began to reach for the jar when it exploded. In a flash, blood was gushing from multiple wounds on Leroy's arm. There was a cut just above his eye; the blood clouded his vision. He just stood, shrieking in terror. His friends fled. Richie stood wide-eyed and shocked, then tore off his armor, helmet and goggles, and flung them into his yard. He opened the gate and dashed to Leroy's side. Richie's memory was racing through the pages of the Boy Scout Manual found in his bookcase, focused on the chapter on first aid. Most of his buttons were torn from his shirt as he quickly removed it. Before wrapping it around Leroy's arm, he tore the hem off, wrapped and knotted it around his upper arm. He picked up a loose tree branch nearby and broke off a piece the thickness of his finger. He stuck it into the knotted strip and twisted it until the blood flowing from all the cuts on Leroy's arm was almost completely stopped. He wiped the blood from Leroy's eye with his hand, all the while speaking in a soothing voice, trying to calm him. Leroy was still screaming; there was a lot of blood.

Richie led Leroy to his back door. He knocked loudly until Leroy's mother opened the door. Her hands flew to her cheeks as she began screaming.

Richie calmed her, quickly explaining what had happened. She turned, removed and tossed her apron over the back of a kitchen chair and took a key from a hook behind the door. They led Leroy, now sobbing, to Mr. Marlow's old pickup truck. Richie watched as they headed down the street toward the hospital. He hoped Leroy would be all right.

Richie returned home and snuck in through his back door, hoping to avoid gramma; the sight of the blood on him was sure to get a frantic reaction. Gramma was in the kitchen, cleaning the stove, making enough noise to cover his descent down the basement stairs. He washed the blood off himself and put his patriot uniform to soak in the laundry tub. He dried himself with a used towel from the laundry chute, put on slightly soiled pants and shirt, and then went up to his room. On the way past, gramma didn't notice a thing. Climbing the stairs, his legs grew heavy and weak. He felt cold, but sweated profusely. He fell on his bed, got up and slipped under the covers, shivering. There had been so much blood. He hoped that Leroy was all right. Gramma's call to supper woke him.

Later that evening, Richie lay on his bed reading a Hardy Boy's Mystery. Through his open door he could hear someone on the front porch, knocking. There were voices speaking in low tones through the screen door. The door opened and closed, the voices moved into the living room. One of the voices sounded like Mrs. Marlow. Gramma called from the foot of the stairs, "Richie, come down, someone wants to see you." Richie counted all fifteen steps going down. He didn't know what to expect. Richie stopped and stood in the arched entry of the living room. Gramma was holding aloft his shirt. It was clean, all the buttons were sewn on, and a hem had been stitched on neatly with a sewing machine. "Richie, is this your shirt?" gramma asked. "Yes, gramma," Richie replied, his voice barely audible, his head down. "Why didn't you tell me what happened, Richie?" gramma asked. "Wasn't much to tell, it was over so quick," Richie said. Mrs. Marlow, seated on the couch, was smiling. "You saved his arm Richie, maybe his life, although I don't know why since he always picks on you." Gramma sat down in her rocker. "Richie, you never told me Leroy picks on you," gramma said. "Well, gramma, that's just Leroy being Leroy," Richie said. Mrs. Marlow got up, came over to Richie and gave him a big hug. "I'll make sure Leroy doesn't bother you any more, Richie," she said. "That's okay, Mrs. Marlow, don't say anything. We have fun, sometimes," Richie said, and then thought, "Someday, I hope."

Gramma sat back in her rocker. A small tear formed in the corner of each eye as she watched and listened. She smiled. Richie was an extraordinary boy, really no longer little, more and more like his father with each passing day.

7

THE PHOTO SHOOT

Richie wore his safari shorts, shirt and boots. His pith helmet kept falling over his face, even though he had loaded up the headband with tape. He straightened it countless number of times, too busy to be annoyed. He was picking through the archaeological find down the street that was piled up at the curb and waiting for the trash truck. He was looking for treasures. He had moved several boxes, rummaged through them, and then stacked them neatly. He didn't think Mr. Mackey would mind having his treasures searched, as long as Richie didn't leave a mess.

He found it in one of the bottom boxes, an old camera. He popped open the front and extended the lens mounted in a bellows that was torn in several of the folds. Stacked in the same box were several rolls of film in their original boxes. The expiration dates on the end flaps had passed years ago. Richie had remembered reading that film kept in a cool dark place should still be good, even after some time. "The only way to find out," thought Richie, "is to take pictures and see if they turn out." He put the camera back in the box with the film, picked it up and headed home at a brisk walk.

Later, he sat at his desk in his bedroom, turning the camera in his hands, thinking of some way to fix it and pay for developing the film. He went downstairs, found a roll of aluminum foil, a roll of sealing tape and the kitchen shears. Back at his desk, he wrapped and taped the foil around the camera bellows. He figured that the foil would not take any folding, so the lens would have to be left extended. He made a carrying strap of an old belt, opened a box of film and loaded it in the camera. Richie went downstairs, showed the camera to gramma and asked if he could go out and shoot some pictures. She smiled and nodded, thinking that Richie had made up a toy to take imaginary play pictures. The camera simply did not look real.

Walking down the street, looking for interesting things to photograph, Richie knew he had to be very selective in his choice of pictures. There were only twelve exposures on the black and white roll. He had left the other rolls of film home to avoid getting carried away and taking more pictures than he could ever afford to get developed.

Richie smiled. Just last week, in school, they had studied the works of Ansel Adams, whose prints, especially the Grand Canyon, though black and white, were world famous and considered a true art form. Richie was excited. Someday, he thought, his work would be studied as an art form. Richie was so hesitant to waste film and so engrossed in picking out things to shoot, he forgot his roaming limits and ended up downtown. He could see the towering steeple of the old church in Loranger Square, one block east of the business buildings along Monroe Street, and he decided to head for the square. Several lawyers and Richie crossed at the light headed for the courthouse. He thought they had to be lawyers. Who else would wear suits and carry big black briefcases on a hot day? Richie took pictures of the Dorsch Library, the Presbyterian Church, and the County Courthouse. He shot three pictures of each from different angles to avoid showing the railroad tracks that ran right through the center of the square. "Too bad," he thought, "I didn't have this camera back in May. I could have taken pictures of the flatbed railroad car parked in front of the courthouse that carried the huge tank for the Firmi One nuclear power plant being built north of Monroe in Newport.

Loranger Square looked old. He decided it had to be at least as old as gramma. He had three shots left in the camera as he walked down Washington toward Front Street.

Richie stood on the corner in front of Kline's Department Store, and looked at the bank across the street through the camera's viewfinder. A big black car pulled up and the doors flew open. Three men wearing masks and carrying shotguns ran into the bank. Richie hid behind the wastebasket that stood attached to the gray metal light pole near the curb. Several loud noises, like firecrackers, sounded in the bank. The men came running out carrying white cloth bags.

Richie was ready. Crouching low behind the waste-basket, he snapped the shutter, wound the film, snapped and wound again, then used the third shot to catch the car speeding away down Front toward Monroe Street. Alarm bells were ringing and people were running out of the bank. A patrol car screeched up seconds later. The Police Department was only two blocks away. Richie stood across the street and watched. A man with a big camera came running by, stopping to shoot pictures of the bank and views up and down each of the streets. More police cars were arriving by the minute. Officers were scurrying around inter-viewing witnesses, some holding back curious bystanders. No one paid any attention to Richie.

The man with the camera stopped near Richie to reload his camera. Richie recognized him as Elgin Payer, the photographer for the Monroe Evening News. Whenever he did a photo series in the paper, they put in a small picture insert of him so readers would know who did the work. Richie tugged on Mr. Payer's sleeve. Mr. Payer looked down and smiled, "Sorry son, can't talk to you now, there is too much going on."

"Sir, I got pictures of the bank robbers," Richie said as he held up his camera.

Mr. Payer smiled, "Sure son, you took some play pictures, right?"

Richie put on his serious face, like he often had to do with gramma so she would listen. "Mr. Payer, this is a real camera. It doesn't look like much because I had to fix it up a little, but its got real film in it."

The smile faded from Mr. Payer's face. "Are you serious? Real film in there?"

"Yes sir," replied Richie.

Mr. Payer stepped to the curb and scanned the policemen across the street. He began frantically waving until he got the attention of an officer. He yelled "Jim!" pointed to one of the detectives, and then motioned to send him over. Mr. Payer and the detective huddled and spoke in low tones, both glancing over at Richie several times. Mr. Payer turned to Richie and asked, "What's your name, son?"

"Richie Spencer, Sir."

"Bob's son," Mr. Payer said quietly to Jim. "Well, Richie, how would you like to go to the newspaper office with us? We will see what pictures, if any, are in that camera," Mr. Payer said.

Richie's face lit up, "That would be great." After pausing, he added sadly, "But I don't have any money to pay for the developing." He didn't mention how old the film was.

Mr. Payer slowly shook his head, chuckling. "Richie, we have a fellow, Sandy, who loves working in a darkroom making things appear on paper with smelly chemicals. He will be pretty excited to see what may be on that film."

Richie sat in a big soft office armchair that swiveled, a bottle of soda in one hand and a doughnut in the other. Annie, a copywriter, the sign on her desk said, had been instructed by Mr. Payer to take good care of him. She frequently glanced over from her typing and smiled. "How we doing Richie?" After two sodas and three doughnuts, he felt he was doing just fine.

Mr. Payer came into the office with Jim, the detective, following. They were both smiling. Mr. Payer carried a large brown envelope and a box. They pulled chairs up on either side of Richie. Jim said, "Richie, we want to thank you. Those robbers shot out all the cameras in the bank and got the money in seconds, but they took off their masks when you took those pictures. We know who they are. We have already found and identified their abandoned car with the help of your last picture. They won't get far!" The detective and Mr. Payer looked up at each other over the top of Richie and both nodded. Jim then said, no longer smiling, "Now, Richie, we think that if we tell anybody about these pictures, it could put you and your family in danger. We can't give you the credit you deserve." Richie shrugged, "That's okay, Gramma would probably be mad if she found out I came downtown. I was supposed to stay on our block. You won't tell her, will you?" Richie asked, wide eyed.

Mr. Payer slid the envelope and box over to Richie. Richie pulled nine enlarged pictures of the square from the envelope. He smiled as he shuffled through them. "Yup," Richie thought with pride, "as good- no- better than Ansel's stuff!" He put the pictures back in the envelope, peered into the box, reached in and took out a camera. It was a brand new camera, not his old clunky one. He turned it over in his hands several times, totally bewildered. In the box, neatly stacked, were at least a dozen new rolls of film.

"That's for you Richie. It's our way of saying thanks. If you take more pictures like the ones in the square, who knows, maybe some day I'll need an assistant," Mr. Payer said, smiling. Richie didn't know what to say, he just smiled in return. Mr. Payer showed Richie how to load and use the camera. Sandy would develop and print his pictures, a favor from one artist to another. They both agreed that should anyone ask, they ran into each other in the neighborhood, which was the truth. Jim moved toward the door. "C'mon Richie, I'll take you home."

Richie got out of the detective's car around the corner from his house. He didn't want to confuse or alarm the neighbors. Gramma listened, arms folded, and looked over her glasses, as Richie told her how he had run into Mr. Payer from the newspaper in the neighborhood. For some reason, Mr. Payer liked him, traded him a new camera and film for his valuable antique one. Mr. Payer also told him to bring any pictures he took down to the paper for developing, free.

"Richie!" gramma left his name hanging in the air.

"Honest gramma, for free. Here's his card. Call him and ask him." Richie slid off the kitchen chair. He had left the envelope of pictures in the garage, to save a lot of explaining. He would retrieve his pictures of the square after gramma gave him permission to go uptown, to use his new camera.

Gramma looked at the card quizzically, not really sure what to say. Before she could gather her thoughts, Richie patted his stomach and asked, "What's for supper, Gramma?" He thought two sodas and three doughnuts aren't much of a lunch.

The Historical Marker in front of the Dorsch Library. The
emblem at the top reads that the City was originally named
Frenchtown in 1785. It was renamed in 1817 to honor newly
elected 5th President James Monroe.

The Dorsch Library building was once the home of Dr. Eduard Dorsch, built in 1850. It was willed to the City of Monroe for library use in 1914. It has served as a public library since 1916, with numerous additions, while preserving many of the original rooms.

The First Presbyterian Church stands beside the Dorsch Library off Loringer Square, across Washington Street from the County Courthouse. The Church was organized in 1820. The present structure was built in 1848. In this church, General George A. Custer married Elizabeth Bacon, a Monroe resident, in 1864.

The Monroe County Courthouse, originally a two story log building, stood from1818 until 1839, when it was replaced with a stone structure, destroyed by fire in 1879. The present courthouse was built in 1880.

8

THE FISHING EXPEDITION

He heard it all from where he was playing in the hall at the top of the stairs. Mr. Mackay had just stepped in the front door, and after mentioning how nice the weather was and that something cooking smelled good, he said, "Emma, I'm going fishin', and with your permission, I'd like to take Richie along since I hate going alone. My grandkids are all so far away, we only get to do grandpa and grandkid things a few times a year. What d'ya say?"

Richie sneaked a peek over the edge of the landing.

Gramma had crossed her arms and tilted her head. That move usually meant no. "I just don't know Mack. You know how I feel about kids by that river."

Mr. Mackay replied, "Emma, I haven't lost a grandkid yet! The water is low enough for Richie to walk across the river right now. Besides, I have fishing vests.

"Fishing vests?" gramma asked. Her arms were still crossed.

"You know how kids usually hate wearing any kind of life preservers around water. Well, I found the answer. It's light, has dozens of pockets and looks like the kind of khaki vests that explorers wear. It's really a life vest. A friend of mine who can't swim likes to fish wading in the river. He is always afraid of stepping into a deep hole, so he found this flotation vest in a fishing catalog. I load up the pockets with raisins, peanuts and jellybeans and the kids fight to wear them. What do you say, Emma?" Mr. Mackay smiled and peered over the top of his glasses.

"Okay Mack, but if either of you comes back wet, a next time is out," gramma said.

Richie was crawling quietly back through his bedroom door silently mouthing, "yes, yes, yes."

"Richie," gramma called.

"Yes, gramma," he answered, stepping to the stair railing, wearing his innocent face. He made all the necessary promises and followed Mr. Mackay out the door.

Mr. Mackay carried the tackle box and lunch basket as they walked the three blocks to the river. Richie carried the rod case. It was lighter than it looked although it was longer than Richie was tall. Richie smiled. He and Mr. Mackay were now leaders of an expedition to seek out species of fish thought to be extinct. Mr. Mackay was the senior professor and Dr. Richie his assistant. The bearers had all run away in fear of the alleged cannibal tribes along the river. Professor Mackay and he had to carry their own equipment. They carried only the bare essentials and wore their survival vests. Mr. Mackay stood at the curb on Front Street, motioning Richie to stay back. Richie's timing was perfect. As he stretched out his arms, all the charging steel elephants that looked like cars born in Detroit stopped and stood short of the line he had invisibly drawn the last time he had crossed. The steel behemoths growled and surged until the explorers crossed, then roared as they resumed their mad dash along their trail. Richie smiled as they went over the Roessler Street Bridge to the far end of the guardrail. The river meant adventure to Richie. Mr. Mackay motioned Richie to follow as he went around the guardrail and carefully made his way down to the river's edge. They walked along the shore a short distance to rough benches mounted on posts facing the water. Richie thought that the cane pole he held was a waste of time. He needed the big rod like those used on the ocean to catch Marlin. After a long five minutes, he felt something and yanked the line to set the hook, like Mr. Mackay had shown him. Richie was almost dragged into the river. Mr. Mackay grabbed the pole as Richie slid past toward the water. The two of them together fought a monster against the current. Richie was sure it was the great white whale rumored to live in Lake Erie. No one ever thought the whale ventured up the river, at least until now. The pole bent in an arc, pulled and bucked until the catch swung into the shallows along the bank. It turned out to be a burlap bag. Mr. Mackay looked inside, made a sour face, carried it to a trashcan and dumped it in. Richie started throwing stones in the river. The stones were transformed into depth charge grenades set to sink into the mud and destroy any enemy submarines cruising in the mud layer.

Mr. Mackay set the fishing poles in forked sticks stuck in the ground. He walked over to Richie and suggested that if he was going to scare the fish, he should learn to throw stones properly. He picked up a stone and threw it, whereupon it skipped over the water five times before sinking. When Richie tried to match the throw, his stone made only one 'splush.' Mr. Mackay smiled, showed Richie how to select a flat stone, hold it with the index finger curled around its edge, then toss it sidearm to send it skipping over the water. After Richie had transferred at least a ton, by his estimate, of flat stones from the bank into the river, he started looking for something else to do. While he ate a handful of peanuts and raisins for energy, Mr. Mackay decided Richie needed a challenge and was ready to cast his bait upon the waters. Mr. Mackay had rigged a spinning rod, tied on what looked like a minnow bristling with needle sharp pointed treble hooks that twinkled in the sunlight. After a few minutes of coaching, almost snagging Mr. Mackay, a tree and himself, Richie finally flipped a cast out into the river. Now he was determined. He would retrieve the bait, fling it almost to the other shore, and then do it over again.

During this time, all fish and other aquatic creatures retreated at least a quarter of a mile up or down the river, spooked by the mushroom eruptions on the surface of the water by the cast bait. All creatures except one large seagull. Like a vulture waiting for the spoils, he circled overhead.

He watched as Richie made a high arching cast, higher than he had ever made before. Then the seagull folded his wings like a peregrine falcon, streaked down, caught the minnow in mid-air, then began climbing away. When the slack line went taut, Richie hung on, the rod making a smooth arc from his hands to the line to the seagull. For the next few minutes, Richie looked like he had a flying model airplane on a string. The gull flew in circles, dove, climbed, looped and rolled. Richie dug in his heels and held his ground. All the while, Mr. Mackay followed the action, mouth agape, like all the bystanders lining the bridge rail, including Sarah and her brother Syl. The seagull began to tire, decided that the minnow might not be worth the struggle, let go and departed in a staggered flight down the river. Applause erupted from the bridge bystanders. Richie took several bows toward the bridge while Mr. Mackay hurriedly gathered all the equipment muttering that it was time to go home.

On the way home, Richie danced back and forth across the sidewalk. He strutted. He was excited and said several times that he couldn't wait to go fishing again. Mr. Mackay smiled, thinking that he himself could wait quite a while. At supper, Richie told gramma and his mom what a great time he had. He recounted the story of catching the burlap bag, learning to cast with a spinning rod and skipping stones. He never mentioned the seagull. The next morning, the whole neighborhood was buzzing about Richie. The story grew with each telling; the Legend of River Raisin Richie and the Seagull.

9

THE BICYCLE

Mr. Mackay wondered how much patience with Richie he would have left at the end of each day. Richie had been coming to watch Mr. Mackay repair bicycles at his shop located in the garage behind his house. Everyday, for a week, Richie wore out poor Mr. Mackay with his inquisitive stream of consciousness. He always wanted to know what Mr. Mackay was doing, why he was doing it, what the names of the tools were, and what he should call each part of the bicycle.

One morning, just a few days ago, someone brought in a bike with bent wheels, twisted handlebars and a broken pedal. The bike had been left in the driveway and had been backed over by their dad's car. Richie asked if he could take it apart for Mr. Mackay, who was busy with a rush repair on a girl's bike. He smiled and nodded. Richie, he figured, couldn't do any more damage to the bike.

Richie had slowly taken the bike apart, wiping each part clean and lining the parts in order on the workbench. He even removed the bent handlebars and the broken pedal. Selecting replacements from the parts' lockers, he installed new handlebars and a pedal with very little direction from Mr. Mackay. Then Richie set out to straighten the bent wheel rims. An old bicycle fork, mounted open end up on the workbench, was used to brace the rim while he worked. Using a spoke wrench, with much patience, adjusting and readjusting, the rims were once again made straight and true. After eating Mrs. Mackay's wonderful sandwiches for lunch he reassembled the bike and it was ready to go. Mr. Mackay shook his head in utter amazement. The quality of the work was excellent.

Ever since he had started assisting Mr. Mackay in the bike shop, Richie had said how much he wished that he could have his own bike. "Someday," he told Mr. Mackay, "I will." He just knew it.

Mr. Mackay knew the family didn't have any extra money, but he had a plan to help Richie's dream come true. One day, while Richie worked, Mr. Mackay phoned Richie's gramma and asked if Richie could have a bicycle. "No Emma, it won't cost anything. Richie has been helping me all week and he has learned enough to build his own bike. I have a lot of junk parts I usually end up throwing away, and he could put 'em to good use. What do you say? Fantastic!"

Returning to the shop, Mr. Mackay went back to work on the girl's bike. "You know Richie, the way I got started fixing bikes was in my uncle's bicycle shop; he let me take a bunch of old spare parts and build my own bike," Mr. Mackay said.

Richie's face slowly lit up with a big smile as he remembered the discarded parts piled next to the shop. "Do you suppose I could do that? Put my own bike together?" He asked.

Mr. Mackay got up and motioned for Richie to follow. They went out and stood by the parts pile. Mr. Mackay nodded and said, "looks like all the parts are there, if they fit." He turned and went back in the shop. He didn't want to make it too easy for Richie, because he believed the best way to learn is do the work yourself. Anything that takes work always has more value, even if it starts with worthless parts.

It took Richie three days of trying to fit parts together. He sorted through frames, wheels, crankshafts, chains, pedals and seats of old bikes that were bent, rusted and greasy. Some parts looked good, but on close inspection were not serviceable. Frustration, skinned knuckles, cuts and scratches were the costs of his creation. When he had it all together, Mr. Mackay talked him into painting the frame and the rusted chrome parts. It would take another whole day for the paint to dry. Richie vowed that someday, he would invent fast drying paint for people who can't wait.

Richie's bike was, in a word: different. The front wheel was smaller than the back, giving a forward lean that he was convinced made it look like it was speeding along, even while it stood still. A long narrow seat, an English racing saddle, as Mr. Mackay called it, gleamed with its polished black leather. The drive sprocket on the back wheel was larger than normal, making it possible for the bike to go faster with less turns of the crankshaft, but this also made it harder to pedal. The chrome wheels, polished and bright, set off the royal blue frame. The handlebars had been painted silver to cover the rust. There were no fenders, front or back.

Finally, launch day was here. Richie rolled the bike out to the front sidewalk. Mr. Mackay brought a step stool and set it next to the sidewalk; Richie would have to use the step to mount the bike since the bike was taller than he was. Mr. Mackay smiled and slowly shook his head. That's the way he had learned to ride. He just got on, pushed off, and pedaled until he had to make the first turn. Back then; there were no helmets, elbow or knee guards. That first turn, and the fall it caused hurt a lot, but nothing got broken. As fond a memory as that was; however, Mr. Mackay made Richie, despite his protest, wear more armor than a knight: hockey equipment that included a helmet, shin guards, knee pads, elbow pads and heavy gloves. Mr. Mackay had insisted, stating that he did not want to have to explain even the slightest scratch to gramma, or better yet, to have Richie's visits to the bike shop cancelled along with his possession of a bicycle.

Richie stood on the step stool and swung his other foot over onto the pedal. He wanted to push right off, but, for several minutes, decided to practice balancing. Finally, he turned his head toward Mr. Mackay, smiled, gave a thumb up, and pushed off. For the first twenty feet, the bike wobbled from one edge of the sidewalk to the other. Richie was concentrating on keeping his balance, trying to steer and pedaling, all at the same time. It was a lot harder than he thought or expected. Finally, the bike began to pick up speed and it all got a little easier. He felt that he was moving so fast; anybody watching would only see a blur.

Then he caught the movement out of the corner of his eye. Mrs. Yates stepped onto the sidewalk in front of him carrying a box of trash to set out by the curb. Richie turned as much as he dared and passed so close behind her that his knee brushed her behind.

She screamed. The box of trash went straight up in the air, narrowly missing her on the way down, and splattering trash all over the sidewalk. Back down the street, Mr. Mackay, watching, covered his face with his hands. Richie got the bike stopped a few houses past. He swung his leg off of the bike, turned it around and walked back to where Mrs. Yates stood in the middle of the walk, still trembling. Richie laid the bike on the lawn beside the walk. "Are you okay, Mrs. Yates?" Richie asked.

Mrs. Yates was checking herself all over, especially the back of her dress. Everything seemed in place.

"I'm really sorry, Mrs. Yates. I hope you aren't mad. If you go get another box, I'll pick up all this trash," Richie said, as he pulled off his gloves. Mrs. Yates went for the box. Richie began to gather all the spilled items in a pile. That's when he found the old coffee can. "No one," he thought, "throws out coffee cans; they make great canisters for storing stuff." The metal lid had been securely taped on. "Why," he asked himself, "would anyone go to all the trouble of sealing a can full of trash?" He peeled off the tape and removed the lid. He stared at the contents in wide-eyed surprise, then quickly snapped on the lid, replaced the tape and set the can beside his bike.

Mrs. Yates returned with the box. She kept trying to help Richie pick up the scattered items of trash, but he insisted on doing it all since he was responsible for the mess. He finished by carrying the box out to the curb. Retrieving the coffee can, he handed it to Mrs. Yates and said. "This fell out of the smashed box and feels heavy. I thought you might want to keep it, you know, like for storing cookies or candy or flour."

Mrs. Yates took the can, pulled off the tape and lifted the lid. She went pale, started to run toward her side door, then turned and came back to Richie. She looked down at Richie, her eyes narrowed into slits. "Richie, do you know what's in this can?" She asked.

Richie looked away and sighed. "Umm, …yes ma'am, I peeked," Richie admitted.

Tears started slowly streaming down Mrs.Yate's cheeks. "Please don't tell anyone, Richie. Okay?" She asked. Richie nodded and began to turn away. She gently put her hand on his shoulder and said, "Richie, thank you, so very much." Richie smiled, picked up his bike and walked back to where Mr. Mackay sat on his porch steps.

The next day, it rained. Richie read some from a Hardy Boys Mystery, recorded the previous day's experience in his notebook, in code, and counted the hours until the next meal. After supper, Richie sat in the living room reading his book while gramma read the Monroe Evening News. She looked around the edge of the paper. "Richie, you know Mrs. Yates down the street? She found a can full of old dollar bills, silver certificates, that her late brother had collected and hid in a box of junk. When she went to deposit them in her savings account at the bank, Mr. Graham, the head teller, refused to take them. He told her that collectors would pay a lot more than face value for them. It's so nice to know that there are still honest people like Mr. Graham. Mrs. Yates can sure use that extra money, especially after losing her husband in one war and a son in another. She has been living on a small government pension and whatever her bachelor brother gave her."

Gramma suddenly put her paper down again. "Oh Yes, Mr. Mackay called. Someone liked the bike you built so much and wanted it so badly they were willing to trade a new one for it. Mr. Mackay hoped that would be all right. The new bike is smaller and will fit you better. He says it's a beauty. He wants you to go get it tomorrow and bring it home. I told him that would be fine. Remember to thank him."

Richie smiled and thought, "Now who in the world would want to make that kind of trade?"

10

THE BOOK

Richie had torn his bedroom apart, searched the living room, including under the couch, looked in all the kitchen cabinets and rummaged through the basement and garage. The book was nowhere to be found. It must be valuable; the copyright was 1927, an early edition. The return date for the book was tomorrow at the Dorsch Library.

When he was much younger, gramma had read *The Spirit of St. Louis* to Richie. The story, written by Charles A. Lindberg, described his life and the events leading to the completion of his historic solo flight from New York to Paris in May of 1927. In August of that year, gramma and grampa had flown up to the Ford Airport in Dearborn to see Mr. Lindberg, whom grampa knew from the airmail service. The decorated national hero, with his famous plane 'The Spirit of St. Louis' had scheduled a tour stop in each state to promote aviation. Gramma recalled how Mr. Henry Ford, a producer of automobiles and aircraft, had actually flown for the first time in his life with Mr. Lindberg. Mr. Ford believed that a pilot who had proven himself flying across the entire Atlantic Ocean could be trusted to safely circle the airport. Last year, on the 30th anniversary of the flight, gramma had taken Richie, Sarah and Sylvester to the Monroe Theater. Jimmy Stewart, gramma's heartthrob of the silver screen, portrayed Charles Lindberg in the movie version of *The Spirit of St. Louis.*

Richie had recently reread the book, noting that it had been rewritten in 1953, winning a Pulitzer Prize. He discovered that the original was published in 1927 under the title *We,* which he then found at the Dorsch Library and checked out on the following Thursday. Now after searching everywhere for it, he feared the worst.

Richie sat at his desk, the contents of his piggy bank neatly stacked and counted. He estimated the book, an original printing, would cost at least five dollars. The coins amounted to exactly four dollars and sixty- four cents. He thought of adding his collection of Indian Head pennies and Buffalo nickels, then decided to make up the difference by collecting empty soda bottles. The refund of two cents each would require eighteen bottles to round out the five dollars. He told gramma he was going bottle hunting. She didn't know about the missing book. Richie hoped he could settle it quietly. Losing a book would probably be a serious offence in gramma's eyes.

The next day Richie put all his change, five dollars and twenty-four cents, in a cloth bag that barely fit in his jacket pocket. He had found more bottles than he had hoped for. Gramma and he walked up Front Street past St. Michael's Church and the Amendt Flour Mill, before turning up First Street. They continued past the Monroe Evening News toward Lorringer Square and the Dorsch Library.

While gramma searched among the rows of books with her list, Richie quietly approached the librarian, Stella, Sarah's oldest sister. Stella had graduated college where she studied English and History. She took the job at the library to be near books, which she dearly loved. Richie enjoyed going over to the Sander's when Stella was home. Sarah was often a little upset with Richie, who could spend hours discussing books with Stella. Richie was convinced Stella had read every book in the library because she seemed to know them all. Stella found conversation with Richie stimulating, because he had read many books that older boys would not have understood. When asked what he would like to do when he grew up, Richie said he wanted to be an explorer, like Marco Polo, Columbus, or Lewis and Clark, and a pilot, like Lindberg and grampa. "Well," Stella said, "Perhaps after you have explored the world, you might become a writer or photographer and share all the things you have seen with people who may never have the opportunity to leave home."

Richie stood at the main desk looking up at Stella. "I think I have a book missing," Richie said. Stella pulled the card file tray in front of her and sat down. Richie told her the title, *We*, by Charles A. Lindberg."

Stella started to search the file, stopped and smiled. "Oh yes, Richie, you left the book at our house last Tuesday. I picked the book up off the floor, and from habit, checked the due date, which was today. I work Thursdays, so I brought it in and returned it for you. It may already be returned to its shelf. I should have told you as soon as you came in."

Richie breathed a sigh of relief and patted the bag of coins in his jacket pocket. He quickly went to the shelf where Lindberg's books stood. *We* was neatly in its place. Richie withdrew the book and went through the pages. The envelope containing the letter he had written to Mr. Lindberg and stuck in the book was gone. He had been undecided whether to mail it. Richie thought it would be a good idea to go ask Stella about the letter.

Stella smiled, and then said, "The letter? Oh yes, the letter in the book. I put a stamp on it and mailed it for you." Richie squeezed his eyes shut tight and mumbled to himself, "She mailed it. Now what will I do?" He sighed, smiled and said "Thank You," offering to reimburse the cost of the postage. Stella refused with a shake of her head, and then added that authors often liked to hear from their readers and she was glad to contribute to the gesture. Richie turned and went to search for a book on flying. He knew that Mr. Lindberg was not just an author or even an ordinary man, but someone who must have great demands on his time. He would probably discard the letter, unopened, into the trash.

Richie had completely forgotten the letter by the second week. Saturday, he was eating lunch at the kitchen table when there was a vigorous pounding on the front door. Richie leaned over in his chair and could see Percy, the mailman, standing on the porch. Gramma went to the door, exchanged a few pleasantries and invited Percy in for coffee. Percy dropped his bag by the door and strode into the kitchen with a handful of mail. He handed a small brown paper wrapped parcel to Richie and piled the remainder of the mail in the center of the table. Gramma poured Percy a cup of coffee and sat down. Percy liked his coffee black, as gramma and mom did. Richie thought the stuff looked and tasted nasty and couldn't understand why anyone wanted to drink boiled bean juice. Percy, without any urging at all, launched into all the latest neighborhood scuttlebutt, which gramma listened to intently. Richie looked down at the package on his lap. No name appeared with the return address, which he did not recognize. He excused himself and went up the stairs to his room.

Richie, his chin on his overlapped hands on the edge of the desk, studied the package, which sat in the center of his desk. The wrapping was perfectly fitted, the ends neatly tucked and glued and the whole package was bound with knotted twine. Someone had spent time carefully wrapping the contents, which felt like a small box. Richie fought the urge to just cut the twine and tear off the wrapper. He patiently unknotted the twine, carefully slit open the glued ends with his miniature sword letter opener, and removed the entire wrapper without a single tear. This way, he could save all of the markings, especially the airmail stamps. He sat back in his chair, staring at a dark velvet covered box with a publisher's name printed on top in gold lettering. It had to be a book. He gently removed the cover of the box and gasped. The book inside was unblemished, and there was the unmistakable new book smell. "Could it really be? It just couldn't be true, could it?" Etched in gold on the book cover was an image of a monoplane and the words, **We by Charles A. Lindberg.** It was a first edition. Richie sat and stared at the book for a long time. He turned the box upside down and let the book slide out. He carefully picked it up and turned it over. Opening the cover, he shook his head in disbelief. He read the inscription over and over. Slanted strokes of a pen had written,

"*To Richie, may your dreams soar and become real, as mine did,*

-Yours-
Charles A. Lindberg

Richie sat and held the book, the same book touched by Mr. Lindberg. He pinched himself to make sure he was not dreaming. Imagine, he thought, Mr. Lindberg actually read his letter and responded by sending this priceless treasure. He slowly began to turn the pages. Stuck in the middle of the book among the illustrations was a small envelope with the flap tucked in. Inside was a note, written in the same slanted hand as the inscription in the book.

Dear Richie,

Thank you for taking the time to write. I will answer all your questions as best as I can.

The original book 'We' was written more as a journal, having been rushed into print as soon as I returned home after the Paris flight.

The book was titled to convey my conviction that it was not I, but We, the Spirit and I, who made the flight. The Spirit was a very special aircraft, one which I helped build, every part of it an extension of me, that part of me that wants to soar and be free. The later rewritten version was properly titled 'The Spirit of St. Louis', which made the flight; I simply went along for the ride.

Thank you for inquiring about our family. All the members are writers, explorers or engaged in concerns regarding the environment and life on our endangered planet. I am fiercely proud that they are not concerned with material things but wish only to serve, as I have always been.

I am delighted to hear that you would rather read a book than watch television. The fact is, we do not own or have a single television set in our home.

In closing, I don't think a slight limp can keep you from spreading your wings and learning to fly. Make your dreams soar!

Yours,
Charles A. Lindberg

Richie put the letter in his square cookie tin along with other valuable things and slid it back under his bed. He replaced the book in the box and went downstairs to show it to gramma.

She was so startled when he placed it in her hands; her eyes went wide in surprise. "Where did you get this Richie?" gramma asked, raising her eyebrows and assessing the innocence of his face.

He quietly said, "Open the book and read the inscription, gramma."

She carefully removed the book from the box and opened it to the title page with the penned note and autograph. A tear formed in the corners of each eye as her face softened and she looked away. She slipped the book back in the box and replaced the cover. She handed it to Richie, got up and went upstairs to her bedroom. Richie hoped he had not upset her. He closed his eyes and slowly shook his head. All he did was show her the book. He turned his head at the sound of gramma coming back downstairs. She was carrying a book tenderly held against her breast in both hands. Her eyes were wet with tears. Wordlessly, she handed the book to Richie. The blue cover was faded. The binding was frayed, top and bottom. A few small bits of silver remained, barely tracing the imprinted title, '*We.*' Richie opened the book to the title page. He gasped when he saw the inscription, written in the now familiar, bold, slanted script.

To my old flying friends John and Emma Spencer, many happy landings,

Yours,
Charles A. Lindberg.
11 August 1927, Ford Field, Dearborn, Michigan

11

AIRSHOW

Richie lay in the grass in his backyard intently studying the insects and bugs in the square foot of ground he had marked off with popsicle sticks and string. Using the big magnifying glass from his detective equipment, he confirmed that every square inch of ground was teeming with life. Holding the nature book in his hand, he asked it, as if talking to the author, "Does anyone else know, or care about these wonders?" He then heard voices through the open kitchen window, and being curious, went in to investigate.

Mr. Mackay was making "mmm" sounds as he demolished a piece of gramma's apple pie and washed it down with sips of coffee. Gramma set a glass of milk and a much too small piece of pie at Richie's place.

She said, "Richie, Mr. Mackay has invited us to go with him and his missus to the air show at the Monroe Airport this weekend, actually, to be part of it. He wondered if you could help him get his antique car ready." Her face was aglow with excitement.

"But just how will we be part of the air show?" Richie asked, slowly chewing each bite of pie to make it last as long as possible.

Gramma and Mr. Mackay looked at each other, laughed with glee and almost in unison answered, "Just wait and see."

Richie walked with Mr. Mackay toward his house while asking a long string of questions. He knew from gramma and her photo albums that grandpa and Mr. Mackay had been partners in owning an antique car and an antique plane, both rebuilt from salvaged parts. Mr. Mackay explained that he had agreed to sell the plane and car when grandpa got sick. Mr. Mackay took his half of the money from the plane and bought out grandpa's share in the car, which Richie knew was kept in the addition built against the south wall of Mr. Mackay's bicycle shop. Every time Richie came back to the question of their part in the air show, Mr. Mackay would answer, "Just wait and see." He told Richie, "The experience of events is always in the unfolding; the joy of the journey is the excitement of the going. Reaching the destination is the end, the finale, so enjoy the excitement of the going." Richie complained that he wished he knew what to get excited about. He could see that gramma and Mr. Mackay already knew and were very excited. Saturday was a long time away to wait and see.

Mr. Mackay's antique car was painted a beautiful deep blue. It was long, with chromed headlights as big as buckets mounted on smooth rounded front fenders, and protected by a sturdy, shiny, chromed bumper. Richie knew all of the parts of the car from his reading. Along the bottom of the sides of the car were running boards to assist stepping into the salon, or passenger compartment, which sat like a small shed with doors and windows near the very rear of the vehicle. Ahead, and separated from the salon, was a wide leather seat, protected by a windshield and a black canvas top, "for the chauffeur and the footman," explained Mr. Mackay. Richie cleaned the windows and polished the chrome trim and spoke wheels while Mr. Mackay attended to mechanical things under the hood. The car, when finished, was put back in the garage.

Friday, gramma phoned Mrs. Sanders, Sarah's mom, and talked to her at some length. She was excited when she hung up. She gave Richie some money to treat Sarah and him to an ice cream, to walk Sarah back to her home and to pick up his clothes for the air show from Mrs. Sanders. Richie was baffled. He asked, "Why would I need clothes from Mrs. Sanders to go to the air show?"

Gramma smiled and said, "Wait and see!"

Richie cringed at the words. Why was everybody so mysterious about going to the airshow? It was frustrating to wait, and more frustrating to wait and see.

Later, in the afternoon, Sarah accompanied Richie to the ice cream parlor on Monroe Street for ice cream sodas. They sat at the marble counter, laughed and chatted as they sipped through straws and ate delicious mouthfuls of chocolate and vanilla ice cream. Sarah mentioned that Sylvester, her younger brother, had gone fishing at the River Raisin with their dad. Sarah had been invited, but she declined, not caring to "drown poor worms and break up fish families." Richie smiled. Mr. Mackay and he would have to go fishing again soon, now that he knew how to cast. He readily recalled the great fishing expedition earlier that summer. Richie paid for the sodas with the dollar gramma gave him, leaving a nickel tip from the change for the waitress as gramma had suggested.

Richie walked Sarah home down tree lined Fourth Street. Each time they left the shade and walked into a patch of sunlight, Sarah's hair turned into a golden halo that framed her face in a way that made Richie's skin ripple with chill bumps, even though it was a warm summer day. She turned her head once and caught him staring. She turned away, but not before he saw her blush. Her eyes were a deeper blue than the sky above. During that single moment he knew that Sarah would always be special to him. They walked slowly, wordlessly back to her house. Sarah was still blushing when they reached her home. Once inside, she thanked Richie for the soda, and then dashed up the stairs to her room.

Mrs. Sanders gave Richie a clothes bag as long as he was tall. She made Richie promise that he would not peek in the bag according to his gramma's wishes. Richie slung the bag over his shoulder and carried it home. Gramma hung the bag on the coat tree in the front hall alongside another, longer clothes bag. She mentioned that she was also going to dress in a special way for the air show. "But why?" Richie asked. Gramma winked, nodded her head and started to speak when Richie threw his hands up in surrender and said, "I know, I know. Just wait and see." He kept mumbling "Wait and see...wait and see..." repeatedly as he went up to his room to finish a flying story about the early airmail.

Supper was swiss steak, mashed potatoes and green beans. The steak was super tender. Gramma had pounded the meat with her special mallet designed for that purpose, using all the energy of her excitement she was trying to contain. The potatoes were so vigorously mashed that not one microscopic lump survived. During supper, mom and gramma were beside themselves with anticipation. They talked excitedly about the coming event at the airport bringing back a little bit of the good old days of aviation. Richie tried to take advantage of the situation by slyly slipping an extra piece of steak off the serving plate. He thought gramma hadn't noticed until she spooned more mashed potatoes and green beans on his plate next to the steak as she continued without pause to converse with mom. Richie ate the seconds with great relish, wishing that gramma would get excited more often at supper.

Saturday morning, after an early breakfast, gramma had Richie take a bath. He protested that Saturday after dinner was bath time. Gramma added some bubbly stuff that "would make him smell good." Why did he have to smell good to go to an air show? What was wrong with the way he usually smelled? Richie wondered why everyone was so excited. He answered himself, "I know, just wait and see." Richie came out of the bathroom wrapped in a big fluffy towel and went into his bedroom. Gramma had laid out the clothes he had brought home from the Sanders on his bed; a white suit with long pants and vest, white shirt, white bow tie, white socks and white shoes. A white cap completed the outfit.

"Everything should fit, Richie. It was Stephen Sanders first communion suit back when he was your age," gramma said as she went out the door and down the stairs.

Richie liked Stephen, Sarah's older brother. He was the kind of brother Richie wished he had. He would be proud to wear anything of Stephen's; although, he wished he knew why he was dressing up so fancy.

Richie stood before the full-length mirror in the hallway near the front door. Gramma always checked her appearance in the mirror, tugging and adjusting clothing or changing the angle of the tasteful, simple hats she always wore when going out. Richie, in his white suit, turned this way and that, admiring himself. He told himself he looked as good as Mark Twain, one of his favorite authors, a picture of whom hung on his bedroom wall. Mark Twain, the pen name of Samuel Clemens, always dressed in white, regardless of the season. Richie wasn't sure what season meant in dress, but he sure liked the way it made him feel...like...handsome. Gramma came down the stairs, smiled, said, "Oh my, how elegant you look, Richie." Richie straightened up taller and looked in the mirror. He sure did look elegant, especially if gramma said so. He looked at gramma as she stepped before the mirror. She wore a light blue dress that had buttons all the way from the ankle length hem to her collar, and wide, dark blue lapels that matched her hat, purse and shoes. Richie thought she looked like she had stepped off the fashion page of the Monroe Evening News.

She asked Richie to bring along a small suitcase that stood near the door. They went out the door, down the stairs and strolled "elegantly" down the street to Mr. Mackay's house. The antique car sat parked at the curb, the dark blue body glistened in the summer sun. Mr. Mackay sat on the porch swing, Stephen and Sarah beside him. Mr. Mackay and Stephen were dressed in dark suits, white shirts and dark ties. Sarah wore a long white dress; a collar of dainty lace matched the cuffs on her long sleeves. A wide red sash circled her waist. Her hair hung in curls like unwound springs that barely brushed her shoulders, on her head was a white bonnet with red ribbons tied in a bow under her chin. Richie thought she looked very pretty, but he was afraid to tell her so.

Mr. Mackay called through the screen door and Mrs. Mackay came out, excitedly greeting everyone. She was dressed as fashionable as gramma, in a dark blue velvet dress with white accessories. They hugged, held each other at arms length, and then giggled like teenagers. Mr. Mackay looked at his gold pocket watch and announced that it was time to go. He and Stephen had put on black uniform caps with shiny visors, becoming the chauffeur and footman.

Upon reaching the car, Mr. Mackay climbed into the drivers seat as Stephan held the door of the salon open for Richie and the ladies. Richie stood back to say he wanted to ride up front. Mr. Mackay smiled and said that the privileged never rode with the hired help. Richie frowned and began to pout. Mr. Mackay smiled, "It's all make believe Richie, like a movie show. We are all like actors playing a part. Maybe you can ride up front on the way home. Now get in and play your part; a rich young man out for a drive with his family." The car pulled away from the curb to catcalls and cheering from the neighbors, many of who sat on their front porches. Richie was confused when the car turned east toward town, not west toward the airport. They drove slowly; people along the street stopped and waved as the car passed by. The car turned south down Monroe Street. Traffic stopped, horns honked, people waved, some applauded, some stood dumfounded, until something had all pedestrians looking upward.

Richie and Sarah stuck their heads out the open side windows of the salon to see what had gotten everyone's attention. An odd looking airplane slowly circled the town. The plane had three engines, one on the nose and one under each wing. He watched the shiny propellers twirl. The noise of its passing, a low rumble, was for Richie, a thing of awe.

He recognized the plane from his reading. It was a Ford Tri-motor, built thirty years ago in Dearborn, north of Monroe. As the car continued south on Monroe Street, it was followed by a panel truck with huge trumpet-like speakers mounted on the roof that announced the air show at the Monroe Airport to begin at noon, a little more than an hour hence. Now Richie was excited, so excited he forgot himself; he leaned over and gave Sarah a hug. Her eyes glazed over and the look on her face made Richie feel weak and queasy. "Why," he asked himself, "does she do that to me? She is just a girl."

The car turned west on Dunbar Road, north on Telegraph, and finally turned west on North Custer Road, which led to the airport. The sound truck followed, playing music and announcing the air show. The road was filled with cars all headed out to the airport. Mr. Mackay turned down the airport access road, past barriers held opened by the security officers. He slowly threaded the car through the crowd amid 'ahhs' and 'ohhs' at the sight of his beautiful car. The car drove onto the paved area that adjoined the small block building that served as a terminal. The Ford Tri-motor had landed and slowly taxied up; the engines turned off and the propellers stopped. The door of the plane opened. A young lady dressed as a nurse, wearing a long cape, helped passengers deplane. They were also in elegant dress. A new car drove in and parked as a modern commuter plane landed. A stewardess in uniform guided passengers down a stair ramp to the ground, they were all in more modern dress. The sound truck announced the theme of the air show, "Commercial Aviation, Then and Now." The air show had begun.

.   The crowds surged through the opened gates and gathered in groups to film the planes, cars and "passengers." Scattered about were numerous parked planes, old and new. Many people lined up for airplane rides, which were offered. The car-plane groups posed for pictures. The most popular attractions were Richie and Sarah, the little rich kids, standing on the running boards of the antique car with the Ford Tri-motor in the background. Mr. Payer, photographer for the Monroe Evening News, was there with his camera. Later, as their posing ended, Richie told gramma he wished he had brought his camera. Gramma went into the car, opened the small suitcase and handed Richie his camera and several rolls of film. She had him change into his own clothes, and then let him go off with Mr. Payer to shoot pictures. Mr. Payer and Richie's dad, also a photographer, had been good friends and had worked together. Richie wished he could remember more of his dad, but knew him only through photographs.

Music began to play through loud speakers across the field. An announcer called out "Ladies and gentlemen, please direct your attention to the bright yellow Stearman Biplane approaching low from the west. We present 'The Sky Dancer,' Joshua Maxwell." The plane circled well west of the field and flew parallel to the north south runway. The engine sound built to a roar and the Stearman began to do a ballet of loops, rolls, wingovers and stalls while trailing yellow smoke. Richie had read of such exhibitions, but could only imagine how the pilot had to operate the controls to make a plane do such things. The crowd was enthralled. Richie watched the whole time, afraid to even blink, afraid of missing any maneuver the bi-plane made.

After the Stearman had landed, Richie went to where it parked. He found Mr. Mackay talking to the pilot. Mr. Mackay introduced Richie to Joshua Maxwell, "The Sky Dancer." As the two shook hands, Mr. Mackay said, "Josh, this is Richie Spencer, Spence's grandson."

Josh smiled warmly, "Your grandfather taught me to fly, Richie, and this plane I fly at air shows was his and Mack's." Josh turned to Mr. Mackay, "Do you think he could have a ride?"

Mr. Mackay turned toward the parked Tri-motor. Under the wing sat gramma and Mrs. Mackay in lawn chairs watching. Mr. Mackay pointed up at the plane and toward Richie. She nodded. Richie was excited. Richie could have exploded with joy.

Josh took a parachute out of a storage compartment behind the rear cockpit, where the pilot flew. Richie sat on the chute in the front cockpit, strapped in with lap and shoulder safety belts buckled so tightly he could hardly move. Josh instructed him on how to release the belts and operate the chute release, "just in case". Richie wore goggles that Josh also provided. The plane was manually rolled away from the people who had gathered to watch. The engine started with a roar and a cloud of smoke. The takeoff was short; the plane lifted and climbed rapidly. It turned toward town, circled once, passed over the field westward, then climbed to a higher altitude. Mr. Mackay smiled, "I guess Richie is going to get a good ride." The plane performed a roll, followed by a big loop. The plane leveled off briefly, and then repeated the roll and loop, before slipping sideways like a falling leaf, losing altitude. It then entered the airport traffic pattern and landed. After the Stearman shut down and the propeller stopped, Richie climbed out, thanked Josh, waved to Mr. Mackay and ran off to find Sarah. Josh walked to where Mr. Mackay stood, peeled off his helmet and goggles, and watched Richie as he ran towards the crowd

Mr. Mackay remarked, "I saw the two rolls and loops, Josh. Richie must have really enjoyed them to have you do them twice." Josh laughed and slowly shook his head in wonder. "Richie asked me to show him one roll and loop. He did the second set." Momentarily, Mr. Mackay was stunned. Then he regained his composure, shrugged and said, "What do you expect, he's a Spencer."

12

HANNAH

Richie was in the alley practicing playing tippy, in preparation for the big match Saturday. Several weeks ago he found the brick, broomstick and several tippys under the workbench. The tippys were eight inch pieces of another broomstick that his grampa had carefully cut into equal segments. Back when he was barely five, grampa tried to teach him the game, but Richie's coordination was just developing and he swung and missed the tippy endlessly. Grampa stored the components under the workbench for a later day. Richie never forgot the good times spent with grampa. It took much practice, but Richie mastered the game in private, then taught it to his friends who enjoyed it so much that Saturday matches were played with a keen rivalry. The game was simple. The brick lay flat on the ground, the eight-inch long piece of broomstick, the tippy, leaned against the center of the brick at about a forty-five degree angle or an angle that worked best for the batter and pointed down the alley. A full length broomstick was struck down on the tippy at the upper end flipping it straight up where it would hang motionless and perpendicular for a fraction of a second while the broomstick was swung like a baseball bat making contact and sending the tippy flying down the alley. Played with others, the longest hit paced off by a scorer won.

Richie was retrieving the tippys when he heard a loud hiss and thud. Something hit a limb in the tree next door; there was a flurry of wings as sparrows scattered. They were followed by Leroy's unmistakable laugh. Richie had heard that Mr. Marlow, Leroy's dad, had given Leroy a BB gun for his birthday last week. Now Leroy was armed and sure to make trouble for the whole neighborhood. "Look Leroy, up on the telephone pole, a big bird," one of Leroy's cronies cried out. Richie quickly moved inside his open back gate and looked up. A bird the size of a dove, one he did not recognize, sat on the very top of the pole. The air gun hissed; there was a puff of feathers and a cry from the bird as it fell to the ground, on its back, wings thrashing. "C'mon," Leroy cried, "Let's catch it and have some fun with it."

"Oh no you won't," thought Richie as he set his face in angry determination. He ran to the bird, shrugged off his light jacket, and in one motion folded the bird's wings, cradled it in the jacket, and ran back in his yard closing the gate behind him. He was carrying his bundle into the garage as Leroy and his friends were shouting directions to each other, searching for the bird behind all of the trashcans and junk piles along the alley fences. After a short time, Leroy's friends began taunting him and telling him that the bird had flown away because Leroy was such a lousy shot.

Richie laid his jacket on the workbench and slowly opened it. The bird was dazed and twitching with one wing drooped. An open patch of wing feathers showed bare skin. The bird was hurt, but how badly he did not know. Mr. Mackay had once raised pigeons and other fowl until the neighbors, one in particular, had complained to the police. He might know how to help this bird. Richie wrapped the bird back up in his jacket, went out into the yard, and up to the back gate. Much to Richie's relief, Leroy and his friends had moved to the next street looking for new targets, in the opposite direction from Mr. Mackay's. He hurried down the alley gently reassuring the bird that Mr. Mackay, who knew everything, would surely be able to help.

Mr. Mackay listened to Richie's account of events as he gently unwrapped the jacket, and held the bird, while talking softly to it in a reassuring voice. He went to a drawer in one of the cabinets lining one wall of his shop. He withdrew a small leather article, which he slipped over the bird's head, covering its eyes but leaving its beak protrude. "That's a hood used to calm pigeons when handling them," Mr. Mackay said. He had Richie put on a welding glove, hold out his left arm, and stand still while Mr. Mackay perched the bird on his wrist. Its claws clung firmly to the glove. Mr. Mackay told Richie to relax and talk to the bird until he returned; he then went in the house.

A few minutes later, Mr. Mackay returned with a book. He sat on his high work stool, referred to the index in the back of the book and then turned pages until he found the correct one. "I was right," he said as he slapped his leg. "The bird is an American Kestrel, usually called a sparrow hawk although it is a falcon. The description of a rusty back and wings means that it is a female.

"Bring her over, Richie, and lets take a look at that wing," Mr. Mackay motioned as he lay the book on the workbench. The bird made no fuss at all when Mr. Mackay opened the injured wing and gently probed it with his fingertips. "From my experiences handling pigeons, I would say her wing is only bruised. The wing needs rest to heal. The problem is, she may not be able to fly well enough to hunt for awhile, which means she could starve or a cat might get her."

Richie looked at the bird quietly perched on his arm. "Could I take care of her until she is well?" Richie asked.

"I suppose so, if gramma doesn't object. Let me call her on the phone and talk to her before we decide to do anything," Mr. Mackay said as he headed for the house.

Richie sat down and rested his arm on the workbench. He knew the bird was light, but his arm felt like it was going to fall off. She sure was a pretty bird. "Can you believe it?" he said quietly, "A falcon is sitting on my arm!" He stroked her breast with his right index finger, wondering if she might peck him with her beak. Richie was pleasantly surprised when she cocked her head and gently leaned against his finger. He was stroking almost to her legs when she stepped up on his finger. Richie thought that those sharp claws would surely penetrate the skin of his finger, but her claws gripped so lightly that he was astonished.

He was softly talking to the bird when Mr. Mackay returned to the shop, amazed at the sight of Richie with the bird sitting on his bare finger. Richie looked up and asked, "Well, what did gramma say?"

Mr. Mackay smiled, turned and went up the stairs into the loft above. He came back down carrying a pigeon cage. The bird was put in the cage, and then placed on a Radio Flyer wagon. Mr. Mackay walked alongside the wagon, steadying the cage as Richie towed it home.

They carried the cage into the garage and set it on the workbench. Mr. Mackay made a perch out of one of Richie's broomsticks and some scraps of wood. Richie learned how to slip the hood on the bird when she was to go on the perch; this was to prevent her from trying to fly so her wing could heal. Mr. Mackay also explained that since her usual diet, sparrows, would not be available, Richie would have to catch mice, grasshoppers and crickets for food. Richie vowed that she would not go hungry.

Gramma came out to the garage to inspect the bird. She quietly stood, arms folded, smiling and admiring the bird. "Have you named her yet?" Gramma asked.

"Named her?" Richie and Mr. Mackay both asked in unison.

"I imagine she is going to get a lot of attention, like someone special, like someone favored. A long time ago, there was a favored woman, the mother of Samuel the prophet. Her name was Hannah." gramma said.

Richie looked at Mr. Mackay, turned to the bird and said, "Hannah, meet gramma, Mr. Mackay and I'm Richie." They all laughed. Mr. Mackay and gramma went out the door as Richie put Hannah in her cage and started to plan on how to find dinner for her.

Richie was wandering about the yard when he heard Leroy and his pals out in the alley. Leroy was shooting sparrows out of the neighbor's tree next door. One of Leroy's victims fell in Richie's yard. Instantly, Richie thought about Hannah's dinner. He scooped up the bird, took it into the garage and pushed it through the bars of the cage. Hannah quickly pounced on it and was eating heartily. Richie sat next to the cage until she finished, talking softly to her while she ate. He felt that the constant cocking of her head indicated that she was listening to him. Before leaving the garage, Richie went to all the windows and pulled the curtains closed. Grampa had hung the curtains, he said, "to keep the curious from looking in and being tempted to foolishly break the law." The fewer that knew about Hannah, the better.

The next day, Thursday, Richie checked out several books at the Dorsch Library on hawks and falcons. He found that hunting with birds of prey was a practice that was thousands of years old. He thought that training Hannah to hunt with him would be exciting, but Hannah hunted for her food and Richie didn't think that doing it for fun would be right. He also knew that gramma would be opposed to the idea. One thing was sure, as much as he would like to show Hannah off to his friends, he knew that he couldn't. He was not only afraid of Leroy finding out, but also the Game Warden. Richie wondered if he was breaking any laws. Mr. Mackay would probably know. He would ask him, maybe in a few weeks.

As the days passed, Richie had to struggle with a dilemma, the sparrows. Leroy was killing them with his BB gun and hiding them in the neighbor's trash. All Richie had to do was tell gramma. Gramma would surely mention it to Mrs. Marlow and the slaughter would stop. On the other hand, Leroy was unknowingly providing food for Hannah. Finally, Richie asked Mr. Mackay what he should do. Mr. Mackay didn't think the sparrow population would suffer any less whether Hannah caught them or Leroy provided them. "Besides," said Mr. Mackay, "sparrows are not native to this country. A wealthy American traveling in England thought they were cute and brought several pairs back to his estates where they escaped and multiplied." Richie felt better after hearing this, and continued to quietly collect them, wrap them in foil and store them in the freezer of the old Coldspot Refrigerator in the basement. Gramma always sent Richie down to put things in or remove them from the freezer, so she would never know about the sparrows.

School was back in session for the fall. The first few days, Richie was the first one out the door with the closing bell. His new shoes with the lifts in them reduced his discomfort and limp to the point he could almost run normally. He ran all the way, across the Roessler Street Bridge, down Front Street to Union, then to his home and Hannah. He spent a lot of time with Hannah. Sarah began to ask what was going on and as much as Richie wanted to tell her, he decided not to make Sarah curious. He decided to start spending more time with the group that usually walked home together. Richie believed that he had patience, but walking home so slowly with his friends tested him to his limits. He knew from the looks Sarah gave him that she suspected something was going on with him. He reassured her everything was okay.

Mr. Mackay came over frequently to check on Hannah's recuperation and was pleased with her progress; he suggested that she would be ready to release soon. Richie did not want to think about it. He had never had a pet. Hannah was no longer put in the cage; she roamed the garage in short flights and perched anywhere she pleased. Whenever Richie entered the garage, he would whistle and she would come and perch on his arm.

Hannah had almost reduced the mouse population to zero, but there were still occasional field mice looking for shelter in the garage. Each day Richie would check her crop to see if she had eaten. He was also concerned to hear that Leroy's dad had confiscated the BB gun because of some broken attic windows. The stash of sparrows in the basement freezer was dwindling. Richie tried to remember where grampa had kept the live mouse traps he used. Hannah was such a pretty bird, he wanted to keep her, but he knew she was a wild bird that was meant to be free, never a pet. Thinking of letting her go hurt with an ache deep down inside, like getting punched in the stomach. He pushed it out of his mind and spent as much time with her as he could.

One Friday after school Richie opened the curtains in the garage to let in the light for Hannah. At the alley window he found himself looking into Leroy's face. Leroy was looking past Richie. Richie turned to see Hannah perched in the opposite window, framed in the light. He closed the curtain quickly, but was unsure how much Leroy may have seen. He barred all the garage windows and padlocked the door that evening. He lay awake all night, listening, and imagining Leroy breaking in and harming Hannah or taking her. At first light, he dressed and went downstairs and out to the garage. He circled the garage, going out to the alley, and to his relief, found everything secure. Inside the garage, he whistled Hannah onto his arm and felt her crop. She had not found any food since he had last fed her. He smiled. Perfect, he thought, she should be hungry. He knew what he must do.

Richie went in the house and decided to surprise gramma and mom by making breakfast. When the bacon, eggs, toast and coffee was ready to serve, he called "Breakfast" up the stairs, picked up the phone on the hall table and called Mr. Mackay. Richie asked him to come over at Ten O'clock.

Mr. Mackay arrived promptly on the hour and Richie invited him in for coffee. When Richie was ready, he asked them all to come into the back yard. He went into the garage and whistled Hannah onto his arm and carried her outside. Mom and gramma, arms crossed over their robes, and Mr. Mackay, sitting on the steps quietly, watched as Richie pitched Hannah into the air. She swooped overhead and circled several times, crying "killy, killy, killy." She then turned southward and disappeared over the Woodcraft Factory. Richie looked away, trying to smile. He was smiling on the outside, but inside he was crying. He went into the garage in case his eyes started leaking.

It was still fall and Richie was outside during recess. He stood alone at the edge of the playground behind

Riverside School, looking southward over the river. He felt empty. When he had tried to read or study, he would think of Hannah and he would lose his place on the page, having to read it over from the top. Last night he had no appetite. At the supper table, gramma kept checking his forehead with her hand to see if he was running a temperature; he looked that pale. He felt empty, very empty. Suddenly, a bird's cry above the playground awakened his attention. He looked up to watch a pair of birds swooping and darting past each other. They were kestrels. A thought went through Richie's mind. "It could be Hannah, but she's probably not around here anymore, these two are probably on their migration to warmer climates." Richie thought, "Still, it can't hurt to try." He raised his left arm and whistled. The kestrels swooped overhead. The largest of the pair turned and glided to Richie and landed on his arm. The entire playground went silent. All activity stopped; everyone froze in place. Sarah, who had been approaching Richie and was concerned about his unusual withdrawal from his friends, stopped and gasped loudly. Mrs. Woodward, standing near the rear doors, recoiled at the sight of Richie. She recognized the wild bird perched on his arm. The bird sat calmly as Richie stroked its breast with the back of his hand. Mrs. Woodward turned and hurried inside after Richie pitched the bird into the air where it joined the other, circling overhead. Everyone on the playground stood motionless and silent, many with their mouths agape. The bell shook everyone from his or her reverie. Soon Richie found himself surrounded by his classmates, all asking questions.

Once inside, Mrs. Woodward entered her classroom with a stack of books she had hurriedly gathered from the school library. Richie had given her the perfect opportunity to introduce her favorite cause, protecting endangered wildlife. She had a special affinity for the birds of prey, like the eagles, hawks and falcons. She could hardly wait to start her lesson. The story of the friendly kestrel would surely be amazing, especially when told by the ever more amazing Richie.

13

CONTRACT AIR MAIL
ROUTE 6

'I was approaching the highest groups of peaks. A white curtain of snow driven by blizzard winds formed a dense mass stretching to the horizons, waiting to engulf me. The mountains now confronted me with steeper and more rugged walls of stone. The sturdy craft bucked and twisted in the turbulence; the wires joining the wings moaned and twanged like a string orchestra searching for a common musical pitch. Visibility fell to a negative number. The fuel gauge, mounted an arms reach ahead of my tiny windscreen, became an indistinct shape in my sweat filled goggles. The roaring wind snatched at my leather helmet as if to wrest it from my head. All that remained of my scarf, tattered and shredded, was the part tucked deep inside the fur lined collar of my leather great coat"*

"Richie, breakfast!" Gramma called from the base of the stairs. Without taking his eyes from the book, Richie rolled to a sitting position on his bed, stood and slowly moved toward his bedroom door. "Richie!" Boomed gramma's voice, "Last call!"

"I'm coming gramma." Richie said as he slid along the banister. He felt for the first step with the toe of his shoe and continued to read. *"I plunged into the opaque cloud of snow which swirled and eddied. My plane thrust upward, crushing me in my seat and threatening to pull my hand from the stick. My boots were held tentatively to the rudder bar by the stirrups. In the next instant we were falling like a stone. I prayed that the wide leather belt securing me to the seat would not fail"*

"Richie, leave the book on the stairs. You know the rule; no reading at the table."

"Yes gramma," Richie said, stifling a moan. He just couldn't leave that poor airmail pilot battling the elements over the mountains. The mail just had to get through.

Richie slid onto his chair after circling around the table to give mom a peck on the cheek. She gathered him in her arms for a mighty hug. When he told her she smelled nice, she laughed and tousled his hair.

There was a knock on the back door with a muffled "Hello." It was Mr. Mackay, coming over for coffee and, hopefully, a piece of gramma's home made pie, muffins or sticky buns. Richie smiled because he knew that Mrs. Mackay usually served breakfast earlier than gramma. The timing was perfect for getting over for Mr. Mackay to enjoy the benefits of both kitchens. Mr. Mackay blew the steam from his coffee cup and tested it with cautious sips.

Richie treasured these Saturday morning breakfasts. Mom didn't open the bookstore on Saturdays in Ann Arbor until ten, and then she'd close early at two. She usually brought back a book or two on the subject of his latest interest. This morning, mom smiled and asked, "what were you reading so intently coming down to breakfast, Richie? It's not often gramma has to call you a second time to a meal."

Richie finished chewing a piece of toast and swallowed as he thought, "Don't talk with your mouth full." He glanced at gramma, hoping that she would notice that he was practicing good table manners. He answered, "I was reading about the early Airmail. Boy, those pilots sure had it rough. It must have been very exciting to be a pilot back then."

Gramma stopped cutting a warm apple pie. She turned to look at Mr. Mackay who returned the glance; he spoke first. "Richie, the reason your grampa, gramma, the Mrs. and I came to live in Monroe is because of the Airmail."

Richie gulped down a swig of milk. "Is that true, gramma?"

Gramma refilled Richie's glass of milk, poured coffee all around, then set out desert plates with wedges of apple pie. She smiled at Mr. Mackay and gave him a slight nod; Mr. Mackay continued. "Hang on for a second, Richie, and I'll tell you the story," Mr. Mackay said between bites of pie and sips of coffee.

Richie's plate was already cleaned. He wished they would quit their jabber and joking to finish their desert. He glanced up at the kitchen clock and started to drum his fingers on the table, until gramma looked his way and raised the "Stop that" eyebrow. He had to concentrate really hard to keep his right foot from toe tapping. He got an approving smile from gramma when he slipped off his seat, cleared the desert plates and silverware, grabbed the coffee pot, and topped off everyone's cup. While it looked to everyone like he was being a good host, he only did it to busy himself. He still had a half glass of milk he had forgotten to drink.

After everyone had finished, Mr. Mackay looked out the kitchen window for what seemed to Richie as an eternity. Mr. Mackay closed his eyes, as if in deep thought, then opened them and began. "Richie, do you remember when you visited Greenfield Village on your school outing?"

Richie nodded while keeping his eyes riveted on Mr. Mackay as he continued.

"Back in 1924, Mr. Henry Ford, who developed the assembly line for building automobiles, thought there might be a future for building aircraft for the developing aviation industry. He had an airfield built on land he owned in Dearborn that is now Greenfield Village. In 1925,Congress passed the Kelly Bill, known as the Airmail Act, authorizing the Post Office Department to contract private carriers to fly the airmail between major cities. Attempts had been made by the Army Air Corps and many government pilots to fly the mail, but they were ill trained and poorly equipped. Many good pilots lost their lives and the general public believed it couldn't be done, at least not on a regularly scheduled basis.

That same year, 1925, your grampa Spence and I were working as test pilots for the Stout Metal Airplane Company, which leased space at Mr. Ford's airport. Mr. Ford could see the demand for airplanes growing, so he decided to join the aviation industry and build airplanes. He then bought Mr. Stout's company.

Mr. Stout agreed to stay on as the design engineer. He had developed an all-metal aircraft with an internally braced wing, something new in those days. The current bi-planes had wires and struts joining the wings, creating drag. The engines of that time could not generate enough power to move the airplane at a respectable speed. Much of the time, airplanes could barely beat the trains.

The single engine Model 2-AT was redesigned as the Ford Tri-Motor, the famous 'Tin Goose,' aptly named because of it's corrugated metal skin. It was so rugged that many of these airplanes are still flying today in some parts of the world. The Tri-Motor is the equipment of choice by the Island Airlines, operating between Sandusky, Ohio and the Put-In-Bay Islands in Lake Erie. Kids ride them every weekday as a school bus between the islands and the mainland.

Even as the Tri-Motor was being redesigned and refined, Mr. Ford's airline began carrying mail and passengers before the official contracts were bid. The airline had such a good safety record that when Contract Air Mail Route 6, known as CAM 6, Detroit to Cleveland and CAM 7, Detroit to Chicago, were awarded, it was no surprise that Mr. Ford was the recipient.

Following the May 1927 flight of Charles Lindberg in "The Spirit of St. Louis," non-stop from New York to Paris, France, interest in aviation and overnight mail delivery went wild, especially since Mr. Lindberg had been an

Airmail Pilot on CAM 2, St. Louis, Missouri to Chicago, Illinois.

The airplanes were very reliable, but problems could develop along the route: fog, freezing rain, storms off Lake Erie, sick passengers and the occasional mechanical problem. An intermediate field was needed somewhere between Detroit and Toledo. A site in Monroe was surveyed. Your grampa and I were dispatched to Monroe to establish the field, staff it and act as relief pilots when required. That's how we came to live in Monroe."

Richie sat wide-eyed, completely enthralled with the amazing story. He had not noticed that his mom had slipped out of the kitchen and gone upstairs. She returned with a square metal box and placed it on the table before Richie. With a glance at gramma and Mr. Mackay, mom said," Go ahead, Richie, open it. I think that both your dad and grampa would say that you are ready for what's inside."

Richie popped the catch open and lifted the lid. Inside were two stacks of books. The ones on top were flight logs, and the larger ones on the bottom were journals. Each book was marked with inclusive dates printed on strips of white tape. Mr. Mackay remarked, "Richie, your grampa's life as a pilot is recorded in those logs." He leaned forward and peered into the box. "I see that his journals are in there too. He often made an entry in a journal before he hit the sack, while the day was still fresh in his mind. I often used to chide him about the novel he must be writing." "No," he would say, "I am just writing down my observations and impressions for my boy, Bob. Maybe someday he will write a novel about us." Mr. Mackay stopped and looked toward gramma and mom, realizing what he had said. They both just smiled, but he still felt bad. Robert Spencer, Richie's father, went to Korea as a war correspondent, but was never heard from again. Mom said, "Take them up to your room, Richie. Just keep them safe.

Richie closed the box and carried it up to his room. Now he could learn more about grampa Spencer and the early days of aviation.

The logs and journals were very detailed. Each flight log entry described where the flight originated and ended, the make and model of the aircraft, the make and horsepower of the engine, the duration of the flight and comments. The space allotted for comments was small. Following many comments was a circled initial J. Richie concluded that the initial must have referred to a journal entry. He quickly confirmed his suspicions. The longer flights all had extensive entries in the journals describing any unusual experiences, emotions or drama that were part of the event. It read like a historical commentary.

There was so much material in the journals; that Richie knew there was too much to read in one night. It would take reading the logs up to a journal entry, then turning to the journal and reading line by line. Richie also wanted to take notes as he read. This was better than a novel. He could hear grampa's voice reading it to him. Now he missed grampa more than ever.

It all began in the earliest days of aviation. The Wrights had flown their 'Flyer,' the first powered airplane, in 1903. A short fifteen years later, the airplane was being used as a weapon in World War I; Grampa and Mr. Mackay had just completed training as fighter pilots when the war ended. They both decided to make aviation their career. The pay wasn't too good, but flying was more exciting than anything else they could think of.

For the next few weeks, Richie slowly worked his way through the log entries and matching journal entries while he kept notes for himself. At the end of some journal entries there were references to PB. Richie asked himself, "Who was PB? Were they initials?"

Reading on, grampa Spencer and Mr. Mackay went anywhere and everywhere they could find work as flyers. They even took up passengers for rides from cow pastures at the edge of towns, "barnstorming" they called it. They flew in air circuses doing stunts; parachute jumps and wing walking. They delivered critical parts to factories, and acted as couriers for messages and documents.

Eventually, they were hired by an emerging aircraft manufacturer to be test pilots. They settled in Detroit, Michigan, staying longer in one place than they had ever stayed before. They both flew the early versions of the Stout Aircraft. They helped inaugurate the airmail flights and pioneered the air routes to Chicago and Cleveland.

They each met and courted the young ladies who would become their wives. They were married in a double ring ceremony in a hangar on Ford Field with the biggest party ever held in Dearborn. Shortly after their wedding, both couples moved to Monroe to establish the intermediate field for CAM 6.

As time passed, and advances occurred in the development of aviation and the airmail service, the Monroe Airport was no longer necessary as an intermediate field. Both Mr. Mackay and grampa Spencer decided to keep their homes in Monroe, now that their children were born, but to continue to travel anywhere there was work for pilots, sending money home, and staying in Monroe when they could borrow a plane and fly in to the airport.

When WWII broke out, they were both commissioned as officers and flight instructors for the Navy. For the duration of the war, they flew with Naval Cadets at the new landing strip paved just west of the original Monroe Airport, established as an auxiliary field for the Grosse Isle Naval Air Station. The Naval Air Station was on the southern tip of the island located at the mouth of the Detroit River where it enters Lake Erie. There were few entries made in the logs or journals during this time. A cryptic note explained that all flight data between the dates of being commissioned, and discharged were 'classified and sealed'.

Following the end of the war, the aviation industry was flooded with pilots, mechanics, and others who hoped to make a living doing what they loved, flying or being around airplanes. Grampa Spencer and Mr. Mackay both had friends in the auto industry that helped them get jobs so that they could support their families and start saving for retirement. During the long summer evenings, they provided private flight instruction, delivered new airplanes from the factories to their destinations and restored antique cars. A pet project was rebuilding a surplus Navy Trainer, affectionately called "the Yellow Peril," which was a Stearman Bi-plane. Every Naval Cadet will remember many anxious moments in the "Peril." Grampa's logs and journals resumed after his discharge from the Navy. The logs listed student names, lessons given and trips flown.

At the very bottom of the stack of logs was a bound book labeled 'Poem Book'. Richie began to read the first entries, then smiled. Of course! The 'PB,' annotated after some jounal entries stood for 'Poem Book.'. In these poems grampa described flying with words that took Richie's breath away. Especially beautiful were the ones about soaring free in motorless gliders. Richie vowed that he would someday fly and soar, to experience the same exhilaration that grampa described in minute, passionate detail.

The journal entries stopped at a page that had a folded telegram tucked in it. The War Department had expressed deep regrets for Robert T. Spencer, Correspondent, Missing in Action in Korea. There were no more entries.

Richie closed the journal for the day, about to lay it down when he noticed the thin strip of tape, tucked midway in the book. The tape marked a page with a simple heading, "John 'Monty' Montrose Sightings". Below it were listed dates beginning in the late 1920's and ending in the 40's when World War II began. The entries simply noted the date, a flight number, the model of the plane, the pilot's initials, and the weather conditions, which were always bad, such as fog, snow, sleet, heavy rain, high winds or poor visibility. Richie took the journal downstairs and showed it to gramma. She smiled and suggested that he go and ask Mr. Mackay. "Can I go right now?" Richie asked.

Gramma nodded, glanced at the clock, and then added, "don't spoil your appetite eating lunch with Mr. Mackay." Richie smiled and went skipping down the walk before the screen door slammed behind him.

In the workshop, Mr. Mackay sat down in his rocker, put on his glasses, and read each entry in the journal at the place Richie designated. Richie began to worry when Mr. Mackay's face turned a pasty gray, like the blood had all drained from it. He had run his finger down the column of pilot's initials until he found the K. M., traced left to the date, and read the entire entry. He shook his head and closed his eyes, as the memories must have come flooding back. He motioned Richie to the chair at his side. "I didn't know Spence had kept track of all those sightings. For years, there were whispers of strange encounters that the airmail pilots had. No one spoke too loudly about them for fear he would be grounded. Pilots were afraid that the operations officer would accuse them of loosing their mind, hallucinating, or breaking under the stress of flying too many flights alone at night.

"It might help you understand if I tell you the story of Monty Montrose. His given name was John and he hated to be called Jack. In those days, John was a popular name and a lot of the men were so named, like your grampa. To avoid confusion, everybody had a nickname, your grampa was 'Spence', I was 'Mack', and John Montrose was 'Monty.'

Before I go any further, I have to explain about the Airmail Routes. The airplanes were very reliable, but flying at night was impossible without a system of navigation; you had to have some way to know your position. There as yet were no radio navigation stations and blind flying instruments available for the pilot. Navigation at that time was 'contact flying,' visual contact with the ground. They had to be able to see and recognize landmarks along the routes. To make night flying of the mail practical, a series of towers with powerful revolving lights, called airway beacons, were installed every ten miles along the routes. They were like lighthouses for pilots. The lights were powered by generators and mechanics on duty made sure they were always in good working order. The beacons could be seen for ten miles or more, even through fog, snow, sleet and rain. When the visibility dropped to zero, as it can do along the lake, the planes were grounded. Sailors can hear a foghorn, to guide them along the shore, but a pilot can't. In severe weather, the pilots would land at the nearest field and put the passengers and mail on a train to finish the trip.

One foggy night, the plane out of Detroit flying to Cleveland had to divert to the Monroe Airport. The pilot had to fly in low along the River Raisin until he located the airport beacon so he could land. We loaded the passengers into a Jitney, which is a small bus, to take them to the train. Monty, the reserve pilot, was supposed to load the mail on a truck and follow the bus, but he had other ideas. He had been idled for many days and he was eager to fly. He had been chomping on the bit like a milk horse without a wagon. Without our knowledge, he loaded the mail in the reserve DeHavilland DH-4 biplane and took off for Cleveland. He lifted off, turned east over the River Raisin and disappeared before we even realized what he had done. The normal route with passengers was to fly the Erie lakeshore south to the Airway Beacon at the foot of North Cape, follow the shores of Maumee Bay east of Toledo then turn east to Cleveland. When passing over the North Cape Beacon, the pilot, if he was running late and was carrying no passengers, could take a short cut. He would turn to a heading of 165 degrees, fly the finger of the cape to its end, cross four miles of water over the lake, and turn to 130 degrees at landfall toward the next Airway Beacon, usually visible just south of the small town of Oak Harbor. Past Oak Harbor the pilot could then fly east to Cleveland. The pilots were all determined to 'get the mail through,' but not to endanger passengers. They had to be able to see the ground to navigate. The attendant at the North Cape light heard the DH-4 pass over the Beacon and make the turn to fly down the cape. He noted the time and recorded it in the log as running late. That was the last we ever heard of Monty. As far as we know he never passed Oak Harbor and failed to arrive at Cleveland. The next day, boats and planes searched Lake Erie and the coastline, but found nothing. The mailbags, however, washed up at the Cleveland Lakefront Airport and were dispatched to

Pennsylvania and New York. Official documents summarizing the investigation indicate that no sign, not a single trace of Monty or his plane, was ever found. Unofficially, pilot lore began to grow about Monty and his plane.

It started a few weeks after Monty's disappearance. An airmail pilot, flying the route, was in big trouble. He was fighting his way through a winter storm at night when his electrical system burned out. He was reading the instruments with a flashlight and had no idea of his position. Frequently, he would look hopelessly into the darkness for the next Airway Beacon, but what he eventually saw was nothing short of miraculous. A foot away from his wingtip flew a bi-plane, a DH-4 with blurred markings. The DH-4 pilot motioned for the airmail pilot to follow him, then banked into a shallow turn. The airmail pilot had to throttle back to avoid outrunning the slower DH-4, but managed to stick with the bi-plane in close formation. They flew through a blizzard of blinding snow and fierce turbulence until the airmail pilot saw an Airway Beacon ahead, it's bright beam cutting through the blizzard like a silver sword. They had reached Oak Harbor. The DH-4 then turned east, flew along for a minute or two, and simply disappeared; it faded away like it had slowly been erased. The airmail pilot finished the flight to Cleveland.

The operations manager, due to the weather, postponed the return flight to Detroit. The next morning, the airmail pilot flew back to Detroit with the morning mail under sunny blue skies. The airmail pilot never mentioned the DH-4 to anyone but your grandfather. If you look in your grampa's journal, you will see the initials K.M. Those are my initials. I knew Spence would listen to my story. He was my best friend. I could tell him anything, and I knew he wouldn't laugh at me or dismiss it as foolishness. When I had finished, he told me a similar story."

"One foggy night he began to wish he had not left the ground. He had missed the North Cape Beacon and was hopelessly lost over the lake, or so he thought. He was about to turn southwest, to find land, any land, when a bi-plane, a DH-4, came alongside. The pilot beckoned him to follow. Spence flew along on his wingtip until they crossed the familiar town of Oak Harbor. The DH-4 then disappeared in a sweep of the Airway Beacon's beam."

Mr. Mackay paused for a time. Richie could tell he still missed grampa. Mr. Mackay looked down at the journal and said, "I don't know how Spence got other pilots to tell him about their strange encounters, but he had a way of making people comfortable around him." Mr. Mackay smiled gently, gathered himself, then asked Richie, "Did you find any other journals or books regarding the list in your grampa's box?"

Richie shook his head and said, "Not yet, but I haven't finished reading all of them. I've been trying to read them in order, just like he wrote them.

Mr. Mackay looked at his watch and noticed it was his usual afternoon mealtime, so he invited Richie in to share lunch. Afterward, Richie called gramma on the phone to let her know he was still there. He also reassured her that he hadn't spoiled his appetite for supper. He thought a bowl of tomato soup and two sandwiches was just a snack. Meanwhile, gramma and mom were busy baking pies for Sunday, along with several loaves of bread for the following week, so Richie was told he could stay with Mr. Mackay until six o'clock. They loved Richie, but baking was sometimes easier without him underfoot.

After they had eaten, Richie helped Mrs. Mackay clear the table of dishes. As Mrs. Mackay began to wash the dishes Mr. Mackay put on his coat and motioned for Richie to do the same. They were going for a long walk. It was an overcast winter day with a deep chill in the air. Fog was forming along the river; and the streetlights glowed within halos that looked like suspended balls of mist. They crossed Front Street carefully between creeping cars, their headlights cutting coned swaths through the swirling fog. They walked nearly to the center of the Roessler Street Bridge. They both leaned against the railing looking west. The fog began to billow and thicken. The air was so damp that tiny droplets slowly formed and then ran down their coats. "Listen Richie," Mr. Mackay said as he glanced at his watch. "That sound is the five-thirty airmail plane to Cleveland."

Richie could hear the drone of an aircraft overhead. "You mean there are still mail runs from Detroit to Cleveland?" Richie asked.

"Certainly. But now they come out of Detroit Metro and go to the new Cleveland Airport. The pilots fly twin-engine Beechcraft with radio navigation. The pilots can land with low ceilings and poor visibility using onboard instruments to make approaches to the runway. They also have radar guidance from the ground to avoid other aircraft. Aviation has come a long way since your grampa and I flew the mail."

As he spoke, the fog kept getting thicker. "This is the kind of thick fog, 'pea soup,' the pilots called it, that continues to be a danger to all aircraft. The pilot has to be able to see the ground to make a safe landing." Richie glanced up at Mr. Mackay as he spoke, and turned his head back towards the river. He blinked, shook his head and blinked again. Above the center of the river, high enough to clear a nearby railroad bridge, he saw some approaching lights. Silently, a fog shrouded Bi-plane took shape. The pilot gently tipped his wings to them. Richie stared open mouthed as the plane passed. The pilot wore goggles pulled down from a leather helmet, and a white scarf that fluttered above a heavy coat with a fur collar. As he passed, he raised a gloved hand in salute. Mr. Mackay turned with the passing craft, smiled comfortably and returned the salute. The aircraft's lights faded and disappeared in the billowing fog.

Richie asked, "Is he going to help that airmail pilot who is flying to Cleveland?"

"What?" asked Mr. Mackay, still looking into the fog.

Richie asked again, "Is the airmail pilot we heard flying to Cleveland going to need help?"

"What help?" Mr. Mackay asked, still looking into the fog.

"Wasn't that Monty in his DH-4 heading for the lake?" Richie asked.

Mr. Mackay, his hand on Richie's shoulder, turned him toward home. He chuckled, "Monty? A DH-4? You have been reading too many flying stories Richie. Let's go home, your gramma will have your supper ready."

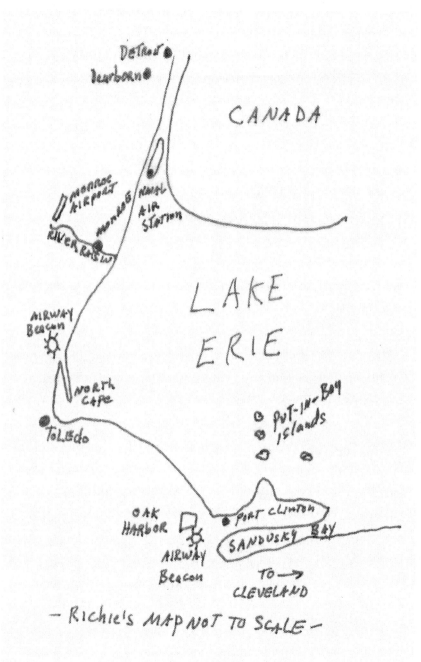

Detroit

Dearborn

CANADA

Stinson Airport

Rumley

NAVAL AIR STATION

RIVER RAISIN

LAKE

ERIE

AIRWAY Beacon

NORTH CAPE

PUT-IN-BAY ISLANDS

TOLEDO

OAK HARBOR

PORT CLINTON

SANDUSKY BAY

AIRWAY Beacon

TO → CLEVELAND

— RICHIE'S MAP NOT TO SCALE —

14

DESERT MYSTERY

Richie walked carefully down his street on the ice-covered walk. He slowed to a stop as he noticed a strange car parked directly in front of Mr. Mackay's, which was where he was headed. The car was an expensive foreign model, very sleek, shiny and large. Mrs. Mackay must have visitors, he thought. She had come from a very wealthy family in Detroit. Her parents had never approved of her marrying Mr. Mackay, a Ford test pilot at the time. Pilots back then, in the 1920's, were considered daredevils; poorly paid and short lived. Richie walked past the house and followed the sidewalk that led to the workshop in the back. He was about to open the door and walk in when he heard voices and roars of laughter inside. He decided to knock instead of barging in. Mr. Mackay, his face covered with a big smile, opened the door. His eyes were wet with tears. His eyes always filled up with tears when he laughed heartily. "C'mon in Richie, I'd like you to meet an old friend of mine and your grandpa's." He turned toward the well-dressed stranger sitting near the wood stove and added, "This is Richie, Spence's grandson. Richie, Meet Crisscross." Richie looked startled, especially when both men broke out in a peal of laughter. "Actually his name is Kristopher Kross, both with a K, but we all thought it was appropriate to call him Crisscross, especially since that was what he did as an airmail pilot in Michigan. He also flew back and forth across the deserts in the southwest for a time. We were having a few laughs recalling some of our misadventures flying the airmail.

Richie climbed up on the stool near the workbench and looked at Mr. Kross with awe. He had been an airmail pilot, like grampa Spencer and Mr. Mackay. Richie remembered that the Airmail created a constant need for bigger, faster planes that helped develop the aviation industry. The Airmail also helped shrink the world through faster communication and transportation. Richie listened intently as Mr. Kross explained that he had flown mail routes throughout the Great Lakes region, but he grew tired of battling the ice, snow, sleet and, especially, the cold. Back then; cockpits were open to the elements with just a tiny windscreen to deflect the slipstream. The early closed in cabins were poorly heated and often leaked. It was common for a pilot to arrive at his destination soaked and frozen if the weather turned ugly. Fortunately for Mr. Kross, a telegram from an old friend invited him to join a new group of pilots flying the mail across the deserts of the southwest. He promptly settled his affairs and boarded a train for Arizona. Through the ensuing years he had served as pilot, mechanic, dispatcher, and, eventually, as a vice president and principal stockholder of a very profitable airline in that region. He recently cashed in all his airline stock and was touring the world. He had intentionally come to Monroe to see his old friends, the Mackay's and Emma Spencer.

Mr. Mackay had made a pot of coffee on his hot plate and filled two chipped, battered mugs, one of which he handed to Mr. Kross. He got a Coke out of his small refrigerator, popped the cap with an opener and handed it to Richie who smiled and said "Thank You." They all sat and sipped as the two men continued to reminisce about places and events, often smiling, nodding, and chuckling as the old stories seemed to rekindle some of their youth.

Richie had just taken a long swig of his soda when he suddenly noted the monogram on the handkerchief that Mr. Kross was daubing his eyes with. It was an X, but an unusual one. It looked like two half circles butted together with small x's inside, like this: x)(x. Richie excused himself and ran home as fast as he could. He burst through the side door and ran past his startled gramma. He quickly explained that he had come home to get something as he scaled the stairs in two's up to his room. He pulled grampa's box of logs and journals from under his bed. Tucked inside the back cover of the last journal was a brown envelope. Printed on the envelope were the words "To John Spencer, to be opened upon my death." Below the words was the mark: x)(x. Richie flew down the stairs and out the door as he said over his shoulder, "I have to go back to Mr. Mackay's, gramma. It's important." She just shook her head and went back to reading The Monroe Evening News at the table.

Richie hurried back to Mr. Mackay's shop. Both men were still sipping coffee and reminiscing, but were no longer laughing. They were more somber as they mentioned the names of fallen comrades who had "gone west." Richie understood the term to mean they had given their lives to be flyers, doing what they loved. Richie went to Mr. Kross and handed him the envelope. Mr. Kross went pale. He sighed in relief when he turned the envelope over and saw that the seals on the flap were unbroken. "Where did you get this Richie?" he asked. Richie told him about grampa's logbooks and journals. Mr. Kross shook his head, smiled, and tucked the envelope in his inside coat pocket. He then picked up the conversation where he and Mr. Mackay had left off, and the old glorious memories once again filled the room.

Richie sat up on a stool, sipping his Coke and taking notes on the back of an envelope. He used the stub of a pencil he always carried in his pocket. Mrs. Mackay came in at one point with a tray of sandwiches and cookies. She gave Mr. Kross a big hug, thanked him for his earlier visit with her and went back in the house. Richie became worried. He had filled both sides of the envelope with notes and was running out of paper. Just then, Mr. Kross glanced at his watch, rose to his feet and handed his coffee mug to Mr.

Mackay. He turned to Richie and asked, "What about you Richie? What would you like to do with your life?"

"Well," Richie answered," I would like to go to college, the University of Michigan like my dad and mom did, and maybe become a pilot, photographer, reporter, writer and explorer." Mr. Kross smiled and shook Richie's hand. He then gave Mr. Mackay a big back slapping hug, opened the door and walked out into cold night air that. he had grown weary of so many years ago. Mr. Mackay stared at the closed door through moist eyes.

Richie waited while Mr. Mackay slowly regained his composure, wiped the corners of his eyes, and blew his nose noisily. Richie finished his coke and asked a couple of questions from his notes. Mr. Mackay cleared his throat and did his best to answer, but Richie could tell that he was still a bit distant, so Richie politely thanked him and said goodbye.

When he reached the front sidewalk, he noticed that the big fancy car, which had to be Mr. Kross's, was still parked in front of Mr. Mackay's house. When he went in the kitchen door, there sat Mr. Kross. Gramma was holding Mr. Kross's hands in hers. She looked very sad. Mr. Kross stood up and gave gramma a long hug. He then glanced at his watch, unfastened it, and handed it to Richie. "Pilots need a good watch when they fly, Richie. Take care of this one for me, okay?"

"Yes, Mr. Kross. Thank you."

Mr. Kross gave him a pilot's salute and turned to leave. He smiled gently as he eased the door shut behind him. Richie tried to put the watch on, but the band was much too large for him. He studied the watch face, looked up and asked, "Gramma, is a Rolex a good watch?" He wasn't sure she heard him, but he decided not to ask again. He just watched as she stood looking out of the kitchen window, trying to control her soft sobs.

A few weeks passed, and another long winter was slowly giving way to the longer days and warmer weather. Mr. Mackay was once again swamped with work. Everyone wanted his or her bicycles and mowers repaired, fine tuned and ready to go. Richie was more than willing to help him just for the fun of working with the tools, but Mr. Mackay insisted on paying him. Then, one day, Richie knocked on the door of the shop, but there was no answer. He waited for a moment and knocked again. This time, he heard a muffled "Come in." Mr. Mackay was sitting in his old rocker, head against the backrest, and his eyes closed. The Monroe Evening News lay on his lap. "Mr. Mackay, are you all right?" asked Richie. Mr. Mackay handed the paper to Richie, and pointed to an article. Richie gasped. A two column header read: **"Aviation pioneer and philanthropist Kristopher Kross mourned."**

The article was long, listing Mr. Kross's accomplishments and generosity, including bequests to numerous Universities and other institutions. Mr. Mackay sat up and told Richie that last month, when Mr. Kross visited, he was returning home from Johns Hopkins Hospital; where numerous tests confirmed that he only had a short time to live. He had stopped in Monroe to pay his last respects to the Mackay's and gramma. While Mr. Mackay spoke, Richie could not help but notice an opened brown envelope on the workbench. It was addressed to Mr. Mackay and had a familiar mark at the bottom: the x)(x of Mr. Kristopher Kross. Mr. Mackay said "Sit down, Richie, I have a story to read to you, an incredible story by an even more incredible man." He began to read from the sheaf of papers in his hand.

"The year I left Michigan I went directly to Phoenix, Arizona. I thought it would be better flying the mail where it was warm. I soon found that the desert heat and the thin air of the mountains created a new list of problems for pilots and aircraft. Frank Marlette, whom you know, had me flying and surveying several routes, for the purpose of marking out safe landing fields with strips of painted canvass. When an engine started to overheat, the pilot could set the plane down, service the machine, let it cool off, and then continue his route."

"When I joined Frank, he had just been offered a private contract to fly the route to Yuma. Frank asked me to survey the route as soon as possible. The next day I took one of the newer air-cooled, radial engine planes and took off after a quick visual check of the weather. The sky was blue, that deep clear blue that is common to the desert. I flew along, marking the map as I went; with possible landing places, the location of the few roads, some deserted mines and a few oilrigs. I figured that I was about an hour out of Yuma when I noticed a sand storm in my path that extended from the ground to a considerable height, a height that I would not be able to climb over. I thought I might be able to reach a road somewhere ahead of it. I went to maximum power, but the headwind increased. I forgot that the winds ahead of these storms are fierce. I felt the grit of fine sand on my cheeks, and I noticed the visibility beginning to fall. The engine started to cut in and out, and I started choking on sand. I had to land while I still had some power, and while I could still breathe. I landed safely on a clear stretch of hard sand. I pulled up to a rock wall that I thought would act as a windbreak. I had nothing to secure the plane except some rocks with which I chocked the wheels. I grabbed my blanket and water bag and took cover in a crevasse. The sand blew for hours; even under the blanket, it was hard to breath. The wind finally subsided with the fall of darkness. I slept, totally exhausted."

"The next morning, I awoke shivering under my blanket. The air was clear but cool. Sand was everywhere; it was even under my clothing, and in my hair under my helmet. My mouth was so dry, the small sips of water I took seemed to evaporate in my mouth: there was nothing to swallow. The crevasse I had hidden in was almost sealed by a mound of sand. A small patch of deep blue showed through a hole at the top. I pushed away enough sand to be able to crawl out. The sunrise was spectacular. The wind had almost completely calmed. I looked toward the spot I had left the airplane. It was gone. I climbed to the top of a rock formation and looked in all directions; there was nothing but sand, rocks, scattered cactus and thin bushes, all the way to the horizon."

"I sat on the blanket, took the map out of my inside coat pocket, shook the sand out of it, and studied it. Taking into consideration that I had been blown east while trying to fly southwest, I figured I was somewhere within a few hundred square miles of the middle of the blankest part of the map. The only marks were those I had penciled in during my flight. It was literally uncharted territory."

"I knew a search would be mounted. When a pilot goes down, he is supposed to stay with his plane because it is easily spotted from the air. Unfortunately, I knew the chances of seeing a human being alone from the air was very remote. My only chance of survival was to find help before my water ran out. I estimated that one of the manned oilrigs was about two days away, on foot, to the northwest. My water, I estimated, should last at least three days if I could conserve it. I decided I would find shade during the day, sleep and rest to conserve energy. I would travel by night, when it was cooler, with the moon and stars to light my way."

"The first day went well. I took small sips of water and mentally built an airplane, piece by piece, to pass the time. The first night's walk was uneventful. At times, I wished I had a compass, but I knew how to use the stars to guide me. Fortunately, that night, their light was bright enough to help me avoid any pitfalls."

"The second day I spent thinking of all the water I had ever wasted. When I slept, I dreamt of all that beautiful Lake Erie water I had flown by on all the mail runs from Detroit to Cleveland. The second night, I saw something on the slope of a sand dune reflecting the starlight. I climbed up the dune, legs sinking up to my knees, until I reached something very shiny and unnaturally shaped here in the desert. When I reached the object, I traced its shape with my hand, straining to see it in the available light. It was something I was intimately familiar with, but my mind refused to believe what it was. Then I felt the corrugated metal rudder of an airplane, a special airplane for me. It was the rudder of a Ford Tri-motor. I spent the remainder of the night, wrapped in my blanket, pressed against the still warm surface of the rudder. I slept fitfully, trying to sort out the reality of it all. Why is this plane here? How did it get here? Is the crew inside, or were they rescued? The dawn finally lit the eastern sky. Perhaps in the daylight I could find some answers to my many questions."

"The plane was well buried. A Ford Tri-motor is no small airplane. The wings span almost 78 feet, and the fuselage is approximately 40 feet long. It stands 13 feet high at the nose. The plane was resting at an angle; nose down. A small fraction of the tail was exposed, possibly by the last sandstorm. I looked for something to dig with, to expose the fuselage, but I found nothing. I tried using my hands, as a dog would use his paws, but the coarse desert sand only made my hands raw. I finally dug with one of my boots, filling it and dumping it like a bucket. I eventually exposed the hatch. I opened it and stepped into the cool, stale air. The forward cabin was filled with sand. There were no passenger seats installed. Wooden cases, their lashings broken, lay smashed open. The crates were filled with bricks, but each brick had its own special compartment. I lifted one from its niche and almost strained my shoulder; it was unreasonably heavy for its size. I knew instantly what I had found: an ingot of gold."

"I sat in the shade of the rudder, thinking of the immense fortune buried here in the sand. I sat for a long time, just trying to think clearly. I thought my vision was beginning to blur when I realized that the wind was beginning to build, and a cloud of sand was fast approaching. On the spur of the moment, I decided to remove two ingots from the plane, which was all I could carry. Each brick, by my estimation, weighed almost thirty pounds. I carried the ingots in the blanket, crawled into a rock formation and spent the day convinced I would surely die, suffocated or buried by the sand."

"The next day finally dawned. The air was calm and cool, and the clear blue sky patiently waited for the blinding, searing sun to roll across it. The sand dune that used to hide the Tri-motor was now a formidable sand mountain. I sat in a small patch of nearby shade, just staring at my nemesis. I was glad I had not decided to weather the sandstorm in the plane."

"Just before dark, I managed to chip out a large mark on the top of a rock spire nearby. I used a rock as a hammer and my pocketknife as a chisel. My hope was to make a distinctive enough mark that I could identify it from the air. I knew there must be a substantial reward for the cargo of this Tri-motor."

"When darkness came, I set out on what I hoped would be my final night of walking. My water bag was empty. I had heard some people say that cactus plants store water, but I also knew that some were poisonous. I never bothered to study which ones had potable water, so I didn't chance it. I put the two ingots in my empty water bag, but the weight began to wear me down more than I expected. I soon needed water desperately; couldn't possibly last another day and night. I buried one of the ingots at the base of three spires of rock. After a few more yards, I thought I could see a faint glow on the horizon. I was afraid I might be hallucinating. The glow was further north than the direction I was headed, but I decided to check it out. Near dawn, I collapsed on the brow of a hill overlooking the brightly lit tower of an oilrig. In my delirium, I could hear men shouting over the clanking of the rig. I buried the ingot in the water bag on a hill behind a shack near a stack of well casings. I crawled down the hill; too weak to even cry out when someone in the drilling crew spotted me. They knew what to do for dehydration; they didn't let me drink all the water I wanted, but gave me only small sips. Later that day, they drove me an hour south to a hospital where I was treated for severe dehydration."

"The next day, Frank came to visit. He was really glad to see me. He explained that a search was made between sandstorms, but with no success. I told him what happened to my plane, and why I had decided to walk out. I never mentioned the Tri-motor. I wanted to investigate that one on my own."

"The following week I was back in the air, one of my first stops was at the oilrig where they rescued me. I brought several cases of refreshments and food for the crew. We spent the night partying. I didn't drink, so I was up early and got to take a walk around the rig while everyone slept. The water bag was where I had buried it. After retrieving it, I helped the hung over cook make breakfast. I took off after a lot of backslapping and promises to stay in touch."

"I flew to Yuma where I rented a hotel room. When I had the chance, I examined the ingot. There were no marks or numbers that usually identify the smelter that processed the metal. I hid the ingot under a floorboard in the closet. Over the next several weeks, I quietly investigated the disappearance of any aircraft in the area from the coast of California to the wastes of Texas. The wreckage or the surviving pilot had accounted for all missing aircraft. The next thing I did was to trace the registration number, remembered clearly marked on the hatch of the plane. The aircraft passed through several owners until it was sold to an airline in Mexico. I had a good friend with official ties with the Mexican Government, and he obtained a list of all U.S. produced aircraft ever registered in Mexico. I found the Tri-motor's number, underlined, with the comment 'Destroyed in crash on remote jungle airstrip.' I found a college student in Phoenix doing library research in the area newspapers. He gladly, for a few dollars, looked for any mention of the disappearance or loss of any transport planes back to the date of manufacture. The plane and its cargo were non-existent."

"I was afraid that taking the gold to any dealer, legitimate or otherwise, would raise questions and the attention of the authorities. I kept the ingot hidden, looking for some way to cash it in. One day, in the newspaper, I read about some gold stock that was for sale. A gold mine was being abandoned. Mining engineers and geologists had little hope there was any more of the precious yellow metal left in the whole mountain. The stock was to be sold for mere pennies a share. I quietly bought up the entire issue. I now owned a mountain with a gold mine."

"After surveying all the air routes over the desert for Frank, I took several months off to explore the desert and try my hand at gold mining. In a new tunnel, I found a vein of gold, very pure and of the highest quality. The U.S. Mint contracted with me to buy the entire production. I knew that such a windfall should be turned to some greater good. Airports, roads, hospitals and schools profited from my good fortune. I bought stock in Frank's airline and became an officer on the board. Investments, many risky, all turned to pure gold."

"During the Second World War, pilot cadets on practice missions reported seeing an antique airplane in the Arizona desert. The authorities mounted a search, finding a partially buried Ford Tri-motor in the desert sand. There was no evidence or sign of a crew; all identification numbers had been obliterated. All instruments with traceable serial numbers had been removed. After all national security measures had been observed; the report was leaked to the hungry press. No one came forward with any information at all. It baffled all of the experts and investigators. It was a mystery plane; it's origin, destination and mission were unknown. It would forever be a mystery of the desert."

Richie sat quietly, unblinking. Mr. Mackey stopped reading and looked off, somewhere in space, or somewhere in time. He put the sheaf of papers back in the brown envelope. He then got up, went over to the stove, opened it and tossed the envelope into the flames.

Richie, stunned, blurted out, "Mr. Mackey, what are you doing?"

Mr. Mackey smiled as he went and sat back in his rocker. "It's a nice story, Richie. Kriss thought you would like it. He asked me to share it with you." Richie looked toward the stove. "But not with anyone else."

"Not even gramma?" Richie softly asked.

"I think she already knows. Maybe someday you can write it as a piece of fiction. Who would ever believe it was true?" Mr. Mackey closed his eyes and leaned his head back. He seemed to doze off, so Richie quietly got up and went home.

When Richie walked in the door, gramma had supper on the table. She stood at the sink, looking out the back window. She was smiling. Leaning against his glass of milk was an envelope with his name on it. Gramma had slit the end open. A letter informed him he had been granted a full scholarship to the University of Michigan by the Kristopher Kross Foundation. Richie forgot that he was hungry. Clutching the letter he went out the door into the back yard facing the setting sun. He solemnly saluted an airman that had gone west. "Goodbye, Mr. Kross. Thank You."

15

THE CLUBS

Sunday was a complete washout. It rained all day, big drops falling straight down from low clouds that seemed to be parked directly overhead. It had been this way every weekend in April, continuing right through to mid May. Richie was on the porch swing, barely moving, watching the downpour. "It is so unfair!" Schooldays were typical spring weather, cool with clear skies. He shook his head. "It isn't fair at all." All the nice days he was cooped up in the classroom, looking out the windows, aching to be outside, doing exciting things. The days were getting longer and there were so many things to do. He liked school, but what he needed was a spring break. Someday when he was in charge of schools, he promised himself that the kids would get a spring break, a long one.

He began thinking about the Sunday afternoon TV show, 'Shell's Wonderful World of Golf' that first aired in April. He had watched it for several weeks now. He had thought it silly at first, grown men hitting a small white ball down long stretches of mown grass called 'fairways', to a very smooth piece of grass about the size of a garage called a 'green' where they took their time using a short club called a 'putter' to knock the ball into a hole. One of the young men, Arnold Palmer, Arnie they called him, had won the first big event of the season called the Master's Tournament. He had grace and charm that made the game look so elegant that Richie was fascinated. As he watched each Sunday, his interest grew. Finally he began searching for several books on golf at the Dorsch Library during his and Gramma's regular Thursday visits. Gramma encouraged all of the neighborhood kids to read books by inviting them along with Richie on the 'Library Day'. Richie had to bring his Radio Flyer wagon to carry the stacks of books home, dropping off his friends and their books along the way.

After he had read all the available golf books, the best, he decided, was by Bobby Jones. Gramma, who had to approve any books he was reading, mentioned that Grampa had played golf. "Somewhere in the house or garage," she said, "was a set of clubs." Richie spent most of one rainy Saturday poking around the basement and garage; however, there were no clubs to be found. As he climbed the stairs to his room to go read, he remembered the attic. Gramma had remarked that she would never go up in the attic because of the bats. She had laughed that Grampa was not concerned about them because he had no hair for them to get stuck in. Richie smiled. He knew bats couldn't stick in your hair, or could they? He wasn't too sure the more he thought about it. In his minds eye he could see gramma as she shook her finger at Richie, sternly saying "Remember Richie, the attic is off limits, it's too dangerous."

Richie took no chances with the bats or any other attic creatures. He wore his long sleeved shirt, long pants, flying helmet, goggles, and gloves. He held his flashlight in one hand and a fish landing net in the other. He was ready to invade the attic. Richie peeked down over the stair railing; gramma was nowhere in sight. There were noises coming from the kitchen; gramma was starting supper. Mom wasn't due from Ann Arbor for at least several more hours. He had plenty of time. He moved quietly to the attic door, unlatched the hooks, top and bottoms and slowly opened it. He held the fish landing net at the ready. Unpainted steps climbed into the darkness. He slowly moved up the stairs, one careful step after another, pulling the door closed behind him. Cobwebs made the stairwell spookier than a vampire movie in the beam of the flashlight. He climbed, unblinking, landing net in front of his face, ready to duck if attacked. Small rain streaked windows in the dormers filtered the weak light from outside. Shadows weaved themselves among the things stacked and scattered about. Richie's flashlight created a cone of dust-laden light that darted around the area, coming to rest on several boxes of books. He immediately wanted to start rummaging through them. He was ready to start toward the books when he spotted the white canvas golf bag filled with clubs.

His memory was suddenly filled with gramma's warning, "Richie, the attic is off limits." Richie decided the books could wait. He crept to the golf bag on tiptoes. He picked up the bag by its handle. It tipped to the horizontal, the clubs clattering in ear splitting sound in the utter stillness. Richie froze in place, looking toward the stairwell, ears straining for any sound. After what seemed like ages, his heart still pounding in his ears, he moved toward the stairs. He had to shift the bag around so the bottom, which tipped at an angle, would go down the stairs first. All he would need now was to dump the clubs out of the bag on the stairs; that would be a sorry end to this episode. He stood at the bottom of the stairs, in the darkness, light off, listening for any warning sounds. Finally, he pushed the door open slowly. The landing was empty. Faint noises came from the kitchen. He carried the clubs to his room, standing them behind the door.

He would have to explain finding the clubs somewhere other than the attic. He would have to get them into the basement or garage, somehow. If he got caught bringing them downstairs, gramma would know he had been in the attic. She would never believe he found them in his bedroom closet. He had been standing in his bedroom doorway while his mind raced through these thoughts. He had turned his head and gasped. Through the gap of the hinges of his door, he could see the clubs! He stepped around the door, quietly picked up the bag and carried it back to the attic door. He gasped. In his excitement, he had forgotten to lock the door. He pulled open the door, set the clubs on the second step and leaned them against the stairwell wall. He closed the door and latched the hooks, top and bottom.

After supper, Richie had gone out to the garage, saying that he was looking for grampa's golf clubs. He poked around the garage, looking for a really good place to find the clubs. He had it all figured out. He would retrieve the clubs from the stairwell, lower them out his bedroom window with a rope, then sneak them into the garage so he could find them. He put a coil of rope under his shirt and quietly slipped into the house. The rough hemp rope tickled. He suffered in strained silence while heading for his room.

Mom and gramma were sipping tea in the living room, talking quietly, and occasionally laughing about something. Richie nonchalantly walked past the living room through the hall, and then forced himself to climb the stairs slowly. He didn't want to attract any attention. He put the rope on the floor under his bedroom window, lifted the window to be sure it opened easily, and then went out to the landing. He peeked over the railing to make sure no one was coming, and crept to the attic door to again unlatch those pesky hooks. He turned the knob and opened the door. He clapped a hand over his mouth to muffle the cry that almost escaped. The golf bag, filled with clubs, was gone.

Richie was sure his hair must have been standing on end. Where were the clubs? He ran to his room to get his flashlight. He took off his shoes, then crept up the attic stairs in his stocking feet. He went up only far enough to peer over the top step. He nervously swept the light around the entire attic, then to the spot where he had first found the clubs. The clubs were not there. The flashlight shook in his hand as the beam slowly swept the room from side to side and top to bottom. There were no bats. Was the attic haunted? He backed down the stairs slowly. He latched the door and returned to his room. He stretched out on his bed, deep in thought. He covered his face with his hands; this whole thing was enough to give him a headache, he thought. Mom called from the kitchen to come down for a snack. He decided that the reason for his headache could be that he was a little hungry. He would figure out the attic incident later. Gramma and mom were having tea and homemade cookies at the kitchen table. Set in Richie's usual place was a glass of milk and a saucer covered with chocolate chip cookies, his favorite.

He was ready to slip into his chair when gramma asked, "Richie, would you go down to the fruit cellar and get a jar of tomatoes for tomorrow?" He nodded, went down the basement stairs and almost fell off the bottom step. Leaning against the washtubs was the golf bag. He closed his eyes, shook his head in disbelief, and then looked again. The bag was still there. He went and touched it to be sure. He got a jar of tomatoes off the shelf and carried it upstairs. He set it on the sinkboard, hoping it was for macaroni and cheese tomorrow. He sat down to munch cookies. Gramma looked over at Richie and smiled. "Did you ever find grampa's golf clubs, Richie?" She asked.

He looked at her with his sweetest innocent face.

"Yes, gramma, I did."

"Where did you find them, Richie?" Gramma asked, still smiling.

Straight faced, he answered, "Right down in the basement, gramma." Richie looked over at his mom. Why did she have her head turned and her hand over her mouth? He took a bite of cookie and hid his smile by taking a swig of milk, which dribbled down his chin, causing all three to break out in wild laughter.

Grampa's Clubs

16

THE COURSE

The day after Richie had found grampa's golf clubs in the basement, he frowned deeper than ever as he examined them. The iron heads were very rusty, the wooden shafts were warped and the leather grips were spotted with mold. He shouldered the bag and went up the stairs. He shouted to gramma, telling her where he was going and went out the back door toward Mr. Mackay's bicycle shop. When he got there, Mr. Mackay smiled as he lovingly picked up and handled one of the clubs. He had to calm Richie and assure him that they were not junk, and that with a little attention and hard work they would be as good as new.

For most of the morning, Mr. Mackay showed Richie how to clean the heads with steel wool and oil, tighten the loose heads with glue, straighten the shafts, and wash and oil the moldy grips. Soon, all of the clubs glistened with a soft satin sheen from sole to grip cap. Mr. Mackay did as little work on the clubs as possible, so that Richie would learn how to repair them. The golf balls in the pockets of the golf bag were all declared dead; not one of them bounced barely a foot when dropped on the sidewalk. Richie was heartbroken.

Mr. Mackay disappeared into the house and returned with a white canvas bag. He reached in the bag, took out a shiny golf ball and dropped it on the sidewalk near the back step where Richie sat, pouting. The sound of the bouncing golf ball got his attention. His eyes widened in surprise when Mr. Mackay handed him the bag.

Richie soon found out that gramma's yard was too small for hitting balls. He spent more time hopping neighbor's fences and searching the alley for balls than hitting them. The next day, Sunday, he couldn't wait for 'Shell's Wonderful World of Golf' on TV. The program was only on from 4:30 until 6:00, far too short as far as Richie was concerned. Afterward, Richie pondered a place to play. Cairn's Field, down the street, had short grass and lots of space, but that's where Leroy and his buddies played baseball almost every day. Gramma would not let him go there alone, and he sure didn't want to deal with Leroy. He went out to the back yard and practiced short chips into a bucket with a niblick, which Mr. Mackay had said was now called a nine iron.

Monday, after school, he decided to go pout on the front porch. While he slowly moved back and forth on the oak swing, a tractor came down Fourth Street. It pulled into the vacant field across Richie's street that was full of overgrown weeds. The tractor then began mowing the grass! Richie stopped swinging and sat frozen in his seat. He smacked himself in the head with his open palm. There it was all the time, his golf course, hidden under the weeds!

As soon as the tractor left, Richie went over with his clipboard, paper, pencil and grampa's long, rolled up tape rule. He measured the length, width and distance from corner to corner. While walking through the field, he noted that the big clumps of grass strewn about and the mown blades of grass were still several inches high. A golf ball would be easily lost in this grass. He soon decided to confer with Mr. Mackay.

Mr. Mackay agreed with Richie that the field would make a nice golf course. He suggested that Richie hire help, like Sarah, Sylvester and some of their classmates to mow the grass shorter and rake it. Mr. Mackay even had a few used mowers he had repaired that Richie could buy at a reasonable cost. Richie frowned. "I only have sixty-three

107

cents saved up," He said. "Not enough to hire help and buy mowers."

Mr. Mackay chuckled. "Richie, you will make more than enough on green fees and memberships to buy several mowers."

"What are green fees and memberships?" Richie asked, puzzled.

Mr. Mackay explained, "People pay to play golf, Richie. They pay for the upkeep of the course through green fees according to how many holes they play. Memberships are when they pay in advance so they can play all they want. Mr. Mackay then asked, "Have you got the holes laid out yet?"

Richie went home and sat down with the stack of golf books he had checked out Thursday from the Dorsch Library.

He focused on a book that his mother had found, a rare 1920 book about golf course design by the famous Scottish architect, Alister MacKenzie. He was the one who helped Bobby Jones design Augusta National where the Master's Tournament is played. Richie got a piece of brown butcher paper from gramma and taped it to the top of his desk. He drew, with pencil and yardstick, the outline of the field using a scale of one-fourth inch to a foot. He then drew, erased, and redrew until he decided that only five holes would fit in the field. Fairways that crossed would not be a good idea unless the golfers wore armor and helmets. He smiled and chuckled to himself, "Would they call that knight golf?" He rolled up his plans and waited for the weekend.

Saturday morning dawned clear and bright; the sun slowly dried the field. Richie, with Sarah and Sylvester's help, staked out the fairways and greens. They buried soup cans flush with the ground for the holes. They tacked white flags cut from a bed sheet onto pieces of old bamboo fishing poles and used crayons to print the hole numbers on them. Near the edge of the field along the alley, there was a foundation floor of fitted limestone paving blocks, where once stood a small building. It was perfect for a small patio overlooking the first tee. Using a hoe, Richie removed all of the weeds that had grown in the joints. Behind the patio, Richie and Syl used scraps of wood and pieces of cardboard to build the concession stand. Finally, they set out to make the signs, get the equipment ready and pass the word through the neighborhood that the golf course would be open for business. The following Saturday, everything was in place.

When they opened for business, the fairways were cut and raked, and greens were trimmed with a borrowed reel type push mower and rolled with Mr. Mackay's lawn roller. Sarah stood behind the counter of the concession stand ready to serve lemonade. On the patio, wooden orange crate seats were set around the big, empty, wooden wire spools found down by the railroad tracks along the new line of electrical poles. Several lines of streamers fluttered from the corners of the concession stand. All they needed now were golfers. That's when Leroy and his buddies showed up. They had brought their baseball equipment and bases. They went right to work setting up a baseball diamond. They collected all the flags from the greens, broke them and threw them in the alley. Richie could only watch, feeling frustrated and powerless. Sarah came over and saw the look on Richie's face. She was really angry. Her eyes looked like two burning coals set in her beet red face. She shook her clenched fist at Leroy and his friends, and then stalked off, taking Sylvester with her.

Richie returned home and watched from his front porch as Leroy and his friends tore up the field with their game. They even helped themselves to the lemonade in the concession stand. Richie had never felt lower in his whole life. His head was down between his knees; small teardrops splashed between his feet. He brought his head up slowly when he became aware of the sudden quiet. The usual shouting and noise of the ball game had suddenly stilled.

On the field had gathered a sizable group of people. Sarah, Syl and Stephen, their older brother, along with some other young men from the neighborhood, all faced Leroy and his friends. Richie slowly drifted across the street and stood in the shadow of the concession stand. He noticed that Stephen and his friends all carried golf clubs. Leroy and Stephen faced each other backed by their respective friends. "Okay Leroy, why don't you take your game over to Cairns Field where you belong?" Stephen said.

"Because I don't feel like it, and besides, we like this better. It's closer to home and we don't have to carry our stuff so far," Leroy sneered, looking to his friends for agreement. "Besides," He added, "Golf is a game for sissies. It's so easy, my mother could do it, any day of the week."

Stephen stepped closer to Leroy. "I play golf Leroy. Are you calling me a sissy?" Stephen asked.

Leroy knew that Stephen was the freshman quarterback on the high school football team. Standing behind him were several of his husky teammates.

"Golf is so easy, Leroy, I'll bet you can't even beat Richie," Stephen taunted.

"I can beat Richie at anything, twice on Saturday," Leroy said as he looked back at his friends for support.

Stephan turned and motioned Richie over. Richie wondered how Stephen knew he was there. Richie walked over reluctantly. "Word travels fast," he thought. There were small groups of neighbors ringing the field.

When Richie picked up a club, his fingers were so weak and wet with nervous sweat, he wasn't sure he could hang onto it, much less swing it. His stomach churned like the agitator in gramma's wringer washer. Leroy and Richie went to the first tee. As they walked, Richie had to look away; all Leroy did was glare at him. Stephen stepped up and flipped a coin. Leroy called heads; the coin showed tails. Richie won 'honors', the golf term for the privilege of teeing off first.

Richie was still shaking as he prepared to hit his first shot. The ball went straight, but he felt like he had no strength. His shot landed well short of the first green. Leroy sneered and strutted up to the tee. He swung the club like a baseball bat. The ball sailed over the green and clear across the street. Stephen walked with Leroy to retrieve his ball. He explained to Leroy about the out-of-bounds penalty. "You drop the ball inbounds and add one penalty stroke to your score on the hole." Leroy finally hit the ball on the green, counting four strokes. He then waited to putt, or knock the ball in the hole, while Richie aimed for the green. Richie had calmed down after Stephen reminded him to relax and concentrate. Stephen had taught Richie the rules of golf and how to play while the course was under construction, and his encouragement meant everything. Richie stepped up, chipped the ball on the green, and made the putt for a three. A three on this hole was a 'par', the French word used in golf to mean perfect.

Leroy missed his first two putts. He was seething with rage and embarrassment. He threw down the putter and stormed off, giving Richie a look that the kids called daggers. Leroy bumped Richie's shoulder as he passed him. He quietly said, "See you later Richie; we're not done yet." Richie's heart sunk down to his stomach. Maybe he could talk Mom into moving back to Ann Arbor.

17

THE LESSON

A week had passed since Richie defeated Leroy in the golf match. Leroy's departing threat, however, had only increased the tension for Richie. He was getting jumpier by the day, not knowing what to expect. Leroy always got even.

Fortunately, Richie's week had not been without surprises. One day, Richie arrived at the golf course and found a coffee can on the concession stand counter with more than a few nickels, dimes, and quarters inside. Richie had never set any green fees, but someone else did. A rough lettered sign said, "HONOR SYSTEM- KIDS 2 CENTS- ALL OTHERS, 10 CENTS." Later, Richie told Mr. Mackay about the coffee can and sign. Mr. Mackay smiled and said, "While you kids are in school, a lot of adults from the neighborhood are playing your course. There isn't another course of any kind around that is so close and convenient. It's also a nice way to practice iron shots, even when someone has only a few minutes to spare, especially early in the morning." After Mr. Mackay had finished talking, Richie happened to glance toward the corner of the shop behind the door. A couple of golf clubs, with what looked like fresh dirt on them, leaned against the wall. Richie smiled.

At the end of the weekend, Richie counted the coffee can money. He set aside half for the course, and the other half was divided in equal shares for himself, Sarah, Sylvester and all the helpers. After the second week, he paid Mr. Mackay for not one, but two mowers. As another nice surprise, Richie had found an old reel type mower on a trash pile. With Mr. Mackay's supervision, it was repaired and cleaned. It was perfect for the final cut of the greens.

Despite these nice surprises, the tension continued to build for Richie. He wondered what Leroy would do for revenge. He knew Leroy would do something and the waiting was very unnerving. The first week the kids were out of school for the summer, it happened. On that particular day, as always, he got up early. He possessed a natural restlessness that seemed to awaken him as the first traces of light slid through his bedroom windows. Because his windows faced east, the first light came before the sun itself could be seen on the horizon. He had climbed out of bed and padded barefoot to his bedroom windows to watch the sun erase the shadows from his golf course across the street. That's when he spotted Leroy. Richie's mind raced through all of the things that Leroy could destroy or damage.

Leroy was a little older and much bigger than Richie, so it would be senseless to go outside and challenge him. All he could do was sit and watch. Richie had his face against the window glass, straining wide-eyed to follow Leroy's every move. He had to rub his eyes with his fists in disbelief at what he saw. Leroy had several golf clubs and a handful of balls. He was teeing up and hitting the balls toward the first green, then retrieving them and starting over again. He wasn't doing too well and his anger was showing. A few times, he looked like he was about to throw his club, but he regained control of himself each time. Leroy had just stepped up to hit another ball when he looked up and saw Stephen, Sarah's older brother, watching from the edge of the field. Leroy began collecting his equipment and headed for home. He stopped when Stephen called out to him; came back and the two of them began to converse. Stephen was older and bigger than Leroy. Richie figured that Stephen could take him easy, or at least tell him a thing or two. Richie watched, and then became bewildered. He even pinched himself to make sure he was not dreaming. Stephen and Leroy went to the first tee. Stephen teed up a ball, then laid some clubs on the ground in the same pattern that he had used when he had given Richie a lesson. Stephen then adjusted Leroy's hands on the club, and, in slow motion, moved him through the swing. Leroy began hitting balls, making suggested corrections and intently listening to Stephen between shots. They hit balls back and forth for some time. Each time, the balls landed in a smaller grouping. After about half an hour, Stephen waved and began walking down the street, toward his home. Leroy gathered his clubs and headed for his own house. Suddenly he stopped short of the curb and detoured to the concession stand. He reached in his pocket and put something in the coffee can.

Richie got dressed and quietly slipped out the front door and sat on the porch swing until he was sure that Leroy had gone inside his house to stay. Richie casually strolled across the street, checking the patio furniture and the concession stand. He worked his way over to the coffee can and peered inside. A quarter lay in the bottom of the can.

For the next week, Richie was up early, sitting by his bedroom windows, watching men of all ages play. Every day, he would also see Leroy hit balls and play a quick round with Stephen. When they finished, Leroy always dropped a quarter in the coffee can.

School was out and none of the kids wanted to get up too early, so Richie always had time to practice and play after Leroy, but before his helpers arrived. On Friday, when Sarah and Sylvester arrived, Sarah drew Richie aside and told him that Stephen wanted to meet him at first light tomorrow. Sarah insisted she did not know why; she was just passing on the message.

The course was busy that Friday. Sarah kept running out of lemonade and had to send someone to the store for supplies. Richie was giving free golf lessons, using Stephen's method. Helping the kids play better made them all want to play more. At one time, there was such a long line

114

of golfers, Richie had Sylvester use a clipboard, take names and act as official starter. Everyone was having a good time.

The next morning, Richie was up earlier than usual. He had not really slept at all. He could hear the Grandfather clock striking each hour downstairs in the hall. Why did Stephen want to meet him early? Did Stephen want to give him another lesson? Would Leroy show up early too? Richie dressed, but carried his shoes. He quietly went down the stairs, counting steps to miss the squeaky one that might wake up mom, or especially gramma with her super hearing. He went into the kitchen and had a glass of milk and a piece of gramma's home baked bread with her strawberry jam. On the rear stoop, he put on his shoes, noiselessly slipped out of the back door and headed across the street to the course patio to wait for Stephen.

Richie didn't have to wait. Stephen was sitting on a crate, leaning against the concession stand and drinking a pint paper carton of orange juice. He handed a carton of juice to Richie and motioned Richie over to another crate seat. Stephen was looking toward the east, pointing Richie's attention to it, and they both sat silently, drinking in the glory of the rising sun. Richie snapped his head around when he heard footsteps crossing the street. His heart skipped a few beats. Leroy was briskly walking toward them. Leroy slowed when he saw Richie, but continued toward them when Stephen waved him over. Richie started to rise to his feet, but remained seated as Stephen motioned him to stay down.

Stephen handed Leroy a juice, then pointed to a crate across from Richie. The three sat very still. Stephen watched the sun slowly climb in the eastern sky; Richie and Leroy watched Stephen.

After what seemed like an eternity, Stephen took a long swig of his orange juice, and spoke. "I've known both of you for a long time. I never did figure out what was going on between you except that now both of you have gotten turned onto golf." He paused then continued. "That's a good thing, because golf is a lesson in life. First of all, as in life, you are not playing against anyone but yourself. It is you

115

against life, against the course. It doesn't matter what the other guy is doing, you have to play your own game, do the best you can. Golf and life both require something called honor. I'll bet both of you hear about good sportsmanship. You are to play fair and be a good loser. Honor is honesty, being able to be counted on to do the right thing all the time. Sometimes the right thing is not the easy thing, or the fair thing. Some time ago, there was a golfer named Bobby Jones. In one tournament, he hit a bad shot and it went in the woods. When he came out, he told the scorer to count two shots. Everyone close enough to watch saw one swing. Bobby said the ball moved at address, which is when you put your club down behind the ball before you swing. He lost the tournament by one shot. "It just wasn't fair," many said. When asked, Bobby said he didn't lose anything because he wouldn't have to live with a lie.

Stephen looked from one to the other. "You both understand what I'm saying?" He asked. Richie and Leroy both nodded. Stephen continued. "The best way to play better is to play with someone who plays well, plays his own game. Both of you play a pretty good game. You both can learn a lot from each other. Today I want you both to play together and don't keep score. Just play for fun. You against the course and yourselves." Stephen stood and tossed his empty juice carton in the trash barrel. "Okay, now shake hands and go play." Then he walked off.

Richie and Leroy both sat and watched Stephen leave. Both felt something bordering on shock and fear. Both almost called out for Stephen to come back, to give them more reassurance that they could deal with their personal demons: Richie with his fear of Leroy, Leroy with his fear of losing to Richie. They stood slowly, did a quick handshake and went to the first tee. They bantered back and forth, each insisting the other go first. Finally, they did a paper, scissors, stone; Leroy won. The kids began arriving, collecting in small groups, amazed at what they saw. Richie and Leroy were playing together and having fun. They were laughing at missed shots, pretending to feint at missed putts and jostling each other, like friends, good friends. After the kids decided there was nothing interesting going on between Richie and Leroy, they all lined up to play. Sarah and Sylvester, watching Richie and Leroy, shook their heads and smiled at each other. Sarah opened the concession stand for business and Syl stepped into Richie's place as manager. Richie and Leroy holed out their putts on the last hole and decided it was time for breakfast. They both headed for their own homes.

"Hey Richie," Leroy called. He then walked over and extended his hand. They both smiled as they shook hands, warmly. "Thanks," Leroy said.

Gramma sat on the couch with the curtain drawn back, looking out the front room window. She watched Richie and Leroy shake hands, like friends would do. "Richie and Leroy have become friends?" She started scanning the sky. "Next thing," she thought, "we will see pigs fly."